Sara's Forever

Drake Wines, Volume 3.5

Chelle Pimblott

Published by Chelle Pimblott, 2021.

This is a work of fiction. Similarities to real people, places, or events are entirely coincidental.

SARA'S FOREVER
ISBN:978-0-6453403-0-3

First edition. November 7, 2021.

Written by Chelle Pimblott.

DEDICATION

To my book bitches without you I wouldn't be writing xx

To my editor in chief, thank you for all that you do and it goes way beyond editing and being a sounding board. Love ya guts!

To my family, thank you for allowing me to write and forgetting to cook for you sometimes. Love you always xx

*****

**Please note **

SARA'S FOREVER

was written by an Australian Author, in Australian English.

As such you may assume there are some spelling errors within, however it's just how we spell things downunder.

*****

Chapter One
SARA

Matt's message comes through immediately, almost like he was sitting at home waiting for my response and it's full of smiley emoji faces.

That's not even the worst part, no, the worst part of it all is that I know he assumes I'm sitting here waiting for *his* response. Even worse than that, I kind of am and that pisses me off!

I'm not that girl! I'm fucking not! I don't sit around waiting for anyone, least of all some guy to *message* or call me back.

I've got a life! A full and busy life at that. I'm not like girls his age, the ones he's used to who have more time on their hands than they know what to do with. The ones who are used to, and enjoy, his hieroglyphic type messages. I want words. I want sentences and dammit, I wouldn't mind some punctuation in there sometimes too!

The problem is, Matthew Phillips isn't just 'some guy' though. Oh no he isn't, on a couple of levels. He's more than that and I'm struggling to admit that to myself.

Another message comes through while I'm debating with myself about all the reasons I should really tell him that this thing, whatever you want to call it, is over but I know I won't.

Matt: *explain to me again why we can't catch up today?*

Me: *so many reasons Matthew.*

Matt: *give me one and make it a good one sexy*

I can give him *so* many reasons that this isn't a good idea that it *should* scare him because it sure as hell scares the crap out of me. So much so that I made a list. It's a damned long one too!

Me: *I'll give you more than one, Matthew.*

1. *You text in emoji's*
2. *You never call, you always text*
3. *You need a girl your own age*
4. *I'm too old for you, we're from two different decades*
5. *It's a phone, it was made for calls as well!*

I hit send and then I wait. When a message doesn't come right back, I assume that my message finally got through. Still, I wait. For what, I don't know what for but I'm waiting anyway.

That's bullshit, I know *exactly* what I'm waiting for. I'm waiting for him to realise that what I said was right and that he needs to go find someone else. Someone who will bring less drama into his life. He knows the main reason why this can't work, I left it off the list for a reason. I don't want to think about it.

After a few minutes of silence I come to the realisation that I didn't in fact want my message to finally sink into his thick skull. I don't want him to find someone else but if I keep telling myself that's what I want, how long will it be before he does exactly what he thinks I want him to do? I want him for myself but I know, *I know*, it can't work.

And *this* right here is exactly why I hate relationships. Not that we really have one, I mean you can't have a *real* relationship when your family and best friend don't know about it! That's the kind of relationship that just isn't worth the pain.

I let the phone slip out of my hand and onto the bed beside me. Just as it hits the mattress, it vibrates, meaning I either have a message or it's ringing. I look at the screen and see his name, M.Flips the third. Why is that his name in my phone? It's so his sister doesn't realise who messages me all damned day.

He's not messaging, he's calling and I know it's because I called him out on messaging all the time but the reason for that is so that I can answer him without telling anyone who it really is.

It stops ringing before I answer it and I let out the breath I didn't realise I was holding. It's not that I don't want to talk to him, it's just that it will be easier to walk away if I don't hear his voice. Seconds later, a text message pops up on the screen and I don't need to be a rocket scientist to work out who it is.

Matt: *Answer the phone.*

Less than two seconds later there's another one.

Matt: *I'm just going to keep calling until you do*

He puts a smiley *and* a damned winky face on the end and before I can even roll my eyes at the excessive usage of emoji's, my phone is ringing again.

"Hello." I try to make it sound annoyed but deep down, I'm happy he called me because I really wanted to hear his voice. It's a sexy voice. Deep, with a rough edge to it and full of amusement, always full of amusement, just like his eyes.

"I do *not* only text in emoji's and I do *not* speak millennial or hipster, my mother and sister would both kill me." He insists but the mention of his sister reminds me of the huge reason this should end. "I enjoy all things retro from the 80's, including but not exclusive to you. And last but by no means least, I *want* to see you again." I can see him counting each point off on his fingers, even though I can't actually *see* him.

"The two biggest reasons for us to stop whatever this is, Matthew, was right there in your opening monologue just now." I sigh.

"And what would those be?" He asks all innocently, like he doesn't know what I mean when we both know exactly what they are.

"One, your Mum." It's my turn to count off points on my fingers.

"She'll be happy for us."

"That's my point, Matthew." I let out another sigh.

"Whatever, that's ridiculous, Sara and you know it! What else?" Anyone else would have sounded annoyed and frustrated but not Matt, he knows the answers to his questions and *still* we're going through them again!

"Your *sister,* Matthew. Remember her? Leila Phillips, you know, my boss and my best friend!" I raise my voice perhaps a little too loudly but I need him to finally understand this, to *get* that this has to end. It has an expiration date no matter what either one of us want or want to believe. This will end and I doubt it's going to be happily.

"She'll get over it." He says it so flippantly, like Leila's opinion and feelings don't matter, like they don't even enter the equation for him but they do matter. They matter to *me* and I know it's going to matter to Leila.

"She matters to *me,* Matthew and if nothing else, that should mean something to *you.*" I sigh once into the phone because this is just not something we're ever going to agree on. "You're just giving me another reason that this won't work." He's proving he's not as mature as he thinks he is.

"Because of my sister? Because I know her and I know once she gets over the initial shock, she'll be happy that *I'm* happy. That *you're* happy, Sara. She'll be happy because we're happy, *together.* I know she'll get over it, Sara, trust me."

"It's not just that she's your sister, Matt, she's more than that." I close my eyes, attempting to hold back the tears I can feel building but not succeeding. My emotions are rarely on display like this and I'm glad I'm home alone now that they are. "She's my best friend *and* my boss! It will complicate my life in more than her simply being, *'your sister and she's not happy'* kind of way." I try to explain, this time it's his turn to sigh.

"So, what you're saying is us, our relationship and me, yes *me,* aren't worth the complication? Am I understanding that right?" He doesn't sound angry, he *does* sound sad and disappointed and that breaks my heart. I'd much prefer he was full on mad at me, I could deal with that but this disappointment makes me feel like an arsehole, when I'm really looking out for the both of us. Long term, this *can't* last.

"Yes! No! Matthew, I don't fucking know, OK? Is that what you want to hear?" I scream into my phone as I hear the crash of my front door flying open. With my phone still in my hand, I walk to the doorway of my bedroom to see Matt slam the door shut and lock it. Then I watch in shock, as he stalks towards me, like a man on a mission until he's standing right in front of me.

I don't need to ask how he got in, I already know because I gave him the key but I didn't give it to him so that he could barge in here uninvited!

"What the hell?"

"Well, you better work that shit out because I'm not going anywhere." He takes my phone from my hand, ends our call and places it on the bedside table.

"Matthew." His name is barely a whisper off my lips. "You can't. We can't." I stutter out because I know we shouldn't, that I should kick him out and take my key back but I can't.

"We can and we will, Sara." He growls, before slamming his mouth on mine and I'm done. I shouldn't be, it shouldn't be this easy for him to get what he wants but it is. Before I know it, the only sounds in my room are moaning, groaning and clothes hitting the floor.

Chapter Two
MATT

I can't help it, when Sara says my full name it makes me hard! Harder than steel, if I want to be all romance book like about it and yes I *do* read them.

I was standing outside her door for most of our phone conversation but that last time she used my full name I couldn't stay outside anymore. I used the key she'd given me and stormed inside to find her in her bedroom. Not tempting at all!

"We can and we will, Sara." I promise her before taking her lips with mine in a bruising kiss. I want this woman more than I could ever properly express to her and I won't let her push me away.

Moans and groans fill the silence, along with the sound of clothes being removed in a hurry and dropped to the floor wherever they land, leaving us in only our underwear. I know I shouldn't do this, I know we should talk things through and sort it all out once and for all but I want her. I mean, I always want her, it doesn't matter whether we're in the same room, same house or same town, I *always* want my hands on Sara.

"Matt." She moans into my mouth as I pull back just enough so that we can breathe.

"Hmmm." I couldn't form words if I wanted to.

"We should talk."

"Mmmm." I wrap my hand in her long dark red hair and pull her head to the side so that I can get to her neck.

"Matt. Ohhhh." She starts to speak again, until I nibble on her neck and then run my tongue over the bites to soothe them. "Mmmm." She murmurs and I know she's got those beautiful green eyes of hers closed tight because she's still fighting me. Fighting *us*. I need her to relax and just enjoy me loving her, I need to get her out of her head. So, I bite harder, then suck and she groans and I can feel her body relax against mine. "Don't leave a mark."

"I know what I'm doing, sexy." I murmur against her skin, knowing that it'll vibrate and when I feel her squirm against me, I smile. "No bruises or marks where anyone else can see them, I know." Then I lick where I just bit and she shivers again. I run my tongue up her neck to her ear, trace around the shell of her ear and then back down, where I sink my teeth into her neck again.

"Matthew." That one word breaks the very thin string I had on my self-control.

"Naked. Now." I grind out, as I reach around her back and unhook her bra.

"You can't force me to."

"Sara, naked, now." I grind out again, this time I slide the straps of her bra off her shoulders and down her arms, the cups are holding onto the breasts that I'm dying to taste because their pushed up against my chest. I take less than half a step away from her and the lace and padding that stops me from playing with her nipples through that lace falls.

I hear the soft sound of material hitting the floor, as I hook my thumbs into the waistband of my boxer briefs and push them off my hips, do a little wiggle and they fall to the ground, landing right next to the lace of her bra. "Now, Sara." I demand, as she stands there, looking at me defiantly, her hands on *my* hips. I don't give her another second to think about it, I slide my hands across her hips, around her back and under the matching lace of her underwear. I squeeze her cheeks in my hands, not so gently and I hear her hiss in a breath. "Tell me to stop and I will." I say quietly in her ear. We both know, that if she says the word, I won't push it any further but we both also know, she likes to give up some of that control she shows to the rest of the world, in the bedroom.

"Ohhh god!" She gives in and rests her head on my shoulder, we both know that's what her movements mean, still I want her to say it. I *need* her to say it.

"Say it, Sara." My voice is low, demanding.

"Matt. More. Please, don't stop." I love it when she begs me.

"Are you sure?" I ask, smiling against the skin of her shoulder when she growls softly and stomps her foot. This is the Sara I love more than any other. Frustrated and begging me for relief.

"Matthew." She draws out my full name for a full thirty seconds, knowing exactly what it does it to me when she says it. "Fuck me now, please." It's the please on the end of her demand that does me in and any chance of me keeping the very tightly drawn string that is my self-control from breaking, is over.

Roughly, I drop the lace covering her pussy to the floor, without taking my hands off her cheeks, I hold on tighter as I lift her up and she wraps her legs around my hips. The heat of her pussy connecting my hard cock making us both hiss in a sharp breath.

"Fuck!" I ground out between clenched teeth.

"Yes! Matt, fuck me!"

"That's the plan, gorgeous." Just not yet.

"Yes!" She screams unintentionally as she sails through the air and lands on her back on the bed. Bouncing once, before I cover her body with mine.

"Guess you should have held on, gorgeous." She doesn't get the chance to respond because my mouth is on hers, demanding entry and she gives it but not before biting my bottom lip first. I smile because she knows she's going to have to pay for that one. "Hands up."

"I want to touch you." She whines.

"Hands. Up." She doesn't fight me, as she raises her hands above her head. "Don't move them. You touch me and I stop, understand?" She nods but I need to hear her agreement and she knows it. I smack her lightly on her breast, right over her nipple and she jumps. "Understand?"

"Yes." That one word is more of a husky breath out than an actual word but I'll take it. For now.

"Good."

"Can I move?" She asks, her voice full of need and her eyes lit with desire.

"Just not your hands. If you can't keep them up there, I'll tie them up." She squirms underneath me at the threat and I know that if I dip my finger through her pussy lips, I'll find her wet and ready for me but I hold off for both of us.

"OK." She nods once in agreement.

Without waiting for her to change her mind, I slide down her body, leaving wet kisses along the way until I reach her breasts. I squeeze them in my hands, pushing them together and licking both of her nipples until her hips are rocking underneath me. As I suck a nipple into my mouth, dragging my teeth across it, I pinch the other one between my finger and my thumb, her harsh intake of breath and her hips pushing up into me, looking for relief tells me she likes it. I take my time, loving each nipple in turn, the entire time stealing glances up to her hands, making sure she's holding on tight to the bedhead.

"Matt. Please, I need more."

"More what, baby?"

"Everything."

"Everything? That's very vague, baby." I smile against the skin of her stomach. A stomach that I know she's not comfortable with because she thinks it's not flat enough but to me, she's gorgeous and I will spend the rest of my life making sure she knows it. I leave soft kisses over her ribs, stomach and when I reach just above her trimmed patch of hair, I stop, breathing in the wetness already soaking the sheets. "What do you need, baby? What do you want more? My fingers, my tongue or my cock. My hard cock that is begging me to let him inside your warm pussy. Are you ready for me?" I ask, already knowing that she's ready for me without even touching her pussy, I can smell her arousal.

"Yes. All of that, please?" Sara, who is always in control, who is always bossy and is always quick with a solution to almost any problem, begging *me* to give her relief, to make her come, is a powerful aphrodisiac.

"I can do all of that for you, baby." I promise her, as my forefinger connects with her clit and I drop my mouth to her pussy. She rides my face as I lick, suck and play with her clit, it's almost violent but I don't care. I push and push until she's coming all over my tongue and face, then I lick her clean as she comes back down. "I'm going to fuck you now."

"Yes." It comes out as a moan. I reach over to her drawers where we keep the condoms and tear one from the strip. Tearing open the packet, I push the condom out and roll it over my cock, then I settle myself between her open legs and rub my cock up and down pussy, driving us both insane. "Matt, please."

"You want me?"

"Yes."

"Are you sure, Sara?" I tease.

'Fuck yes, Matt, please." Her eyes meet mine and I see all the desire and heat there and I need more. More of the physical but more of everything else as well. More commitment and I'm not above using sex to get it.

"I'm not letting you go, Sara. You're mine. Tell me. Admit I'm yours too." I pant out between thrusts, as I push just the head of my cock in and out of her pussy, teasing her with what she could have if she just admits that she needs more than just my body and my cock.

"Matt. More. Please." I lean on one elbow and take her chin in my now free hand and bring her eyes to mine.

"Tell me, Sara. Tell me that I'm yours and you're mine. Admit it baby and I'll give you what you want."

"Matt. I, please." She closes her eyes, hiding from me.

"Open your eyes, Sara. Look at me and tell me you don't want me, that you don't need me. Tell me that I'm not yours. Tell me that we're not worth it, *I'm* not worth it." She can't, I know she can't look me in the eyes and lie to me and so does she.

"I can't." She tries to shake her head but I hold her tighter, forcing her to look me in the eyes and deny me. "Don't make me, Matthew." I don't say a word but my whole body stills, waiting. "I need you Matt. You're mine and I'm yours."

I plunge in one push deep into her pussy and we both sigh in relief. I love this woman and I won't let her lie to me or herself. As long as she feels the same, the rest we can work out. I drop her chin and push myself up on my hands for more leverage and start building us both up to our orgasms.

She reaches up and takes my face in her hands and just as I'm about to tell her off for touching me, she says the three words I've been needing to hear, if not exactly the ones I want to hear her say. They're the three words that mean that we *can* make this work because no matter what happens after them, I *know* that I'll fight for us.

Chapter Three
SARA

"I am *yours,* Matthew Patrick Phillips." It's not quite what I'm feeling. Not quite the three words that are on the tip of my tongue but that's all I'm willing to give. For tonight anyway. My emotions and my loyalty are still battling it out for the rights to rule.

His brown eyes search mine for a second as I hold his head still, I need him to see what I can't say. I know it's not fair but it's the best I can offer for now.

"Touch me." He whispers as he drives his cock into me, holding himself there until I run my hands down his neck, over his shoulders and down his arms. I was expecting him to punish me for moving them, not ask me to keep going. Apparently, we *both* need something tonight. Leaning down, he kisses me, so gently and passionately that it almost brings me to tears. We're always all about the rules and hard fucking but tonight feels different.

He pulls back from our kiss and I miss his lips immediately, I try to sit up a little, chasing his lips but he sits back on his heels, out of my reach and my hands drop to the mattress lost because they *need* to touch him. His hands grip my hips to hold me in place as he continues to drive his cock into me so deep that I'm not sure where I end and he begins.

"Matt."

"Play with your tits, baby. Squeeze them and pinch those nipples for me." He demands and I hesitate for a second before I obey. His gorgeous brown eyes dilate with desire and my lips part, on the verge of a gasp, maybe a moan but not managing to make a sound at all. "Fuck yes!"

His hips withdraw his cock from my body and then pound it right back in, barely giving me a chance to catch my breath and I don't want him to stop.

"Don't stop, Matt. Don't. Fucking. Stop!" I plead, I'm so close to coming that if he stops now, I'm afraid I might just kill him. For real.

"I will if you don't keep pinching those nipples and squeezing those tits for me." I know he's close himself because his voice is strained and he's gritting his teeth. "Fuck me, Sara."

"I thought that was your job?" I pant out, knowing that's going to cost me but I don't care.

"If you can still be a smart arse, then I'm not fucking you hard enough and you're not working those tits enough." He slaps the side of my thigh because he can't get to my butt cheek and I groan.

I don't get a second to think though because his thumb finds my clit and he pushes against it, hard. I pinch both of my nipples hard as a result because I can't. I can't anything. There are no words to put together, no sounds coming out of me, just a gasp of pleasure. He plays me like an instrument and he knows it. He's learned my body like no other guy I've ever been with and that's what makes him so fucking dangerous. It makes him addictive because my body craves him.

Even more dangerous is the fact that he knows it.

"Matt." I growl and I don't know whether I'm growling because I'm pissed off with him or because I'm on the edge, ready to drop into my orgasm and forget the world.

"Come for me, Sara. Now!" His command is what sends me over the edge and I'm screaming out his name as I squeeze his cock as I come, hard. "Yes, that's it. Ahhh fuck!" I barely notice as his hips start moving in wilder, uncontrolled movements as he reaches his own orgasm.

He drops down, resting his head on my breast, which are still covered with my hands but he's holding most of his weight off me by leaning on his forearms. After who knows how long, he slowly withdraws from my pussy and moves around the room to get rid of the used condom.

I haven't moved when he comes back, so he fixes the covers and then climbs in beside me, pulling me into his arms before covering us both up.

"I have to go to the bathroom." I tell him, even as I snuggle into his side, my hand resting on his chest.

"I know but you can cuddle for a minute." More demands! I wish I cared to put him in his place right now but I don't.

After a few minutes, I push away from him and fold back the covers so that I can make my way to the bathroom. He doesn't argue or try to pull me back into bed with him, he lets me go do what I need to and I love him for it. It scares me at the same time though because it feels so domestic, so intimate that he knows exactly what I need to do before I can relax and cuddle up with him. Maybe even fall asleep.

When I get back into the bedroom, I study him as I make my back to the bed. He's lying there, eyes closed, the covers mostly covering him, with one arm outstretched, waiting for me to lay on it so that he can wrap it around me. The hand resting on his chest and I know that one will eventually be doing one of a few things. It'll be holding my hand, running through my hair or holding my legs across his body. There are other options but these are the most common.

"Don't just stand there, get back into bed with me."

"Pushy bastard."

"That's me. Now get here. I want my after sex cuddles now, please." He hasn't opened his eyes but he's wearing a sexy as hell smirk, like he's confident that's what I want too. A cuddle. Little does he know that's exactly what I want, in fact, I crave it and his touch most days.

"You know, you can't just force your way into my house and then start bossing me around." I lecture him, even as I crawl into my bed and let myself get wrapped up in his arms and around his body. He has the good grace to *not* laugh at me or question me. "I gave you a key for emergencies and for when you're *invited* in, not so that you can force your way in here."

"Are you complaining, gorgeous?" I rest my chin on my hand that is spread across his fuzzy chest, to look at his face. His eyes are still closed and he has a small smile on his face that makes me believe he's a very satisfied man.

"I never said it was a complaint, I said you didn't have *permission* to enter my humble abode whenever you feel like it."

"Those are some fancy words for a woman who wants nothing more than sleep right now."

"Wow, arrogant much?" I scoff and start to pull away from him.

"Not arrogant, I just know you and I *know* it's time for a nap before we order in some food because even though you cook all day, there's never anything decent to eat in this house. No ingredients to even throw together for something to eat, other than a quick breakfast and some coffee."

"That's rude!" Not untrue but still rude. Most people I know that cook and feed people all day, don't have much in their own cupboards or fridge. Leila being the one exception to that rule because she can *always* throw together a great meal no matter the time of day.

"Stop it. Don't bring her in here right now. Please." He speaks so quietly that if it wasn't silent in the room, I might have missed it.

"I didn't say a thing." I protest.

"You didn't have to, Sara. I felt your body stiffen and I knew exactly who you were thinking about. Please, just for tonight, can we leave her out of this relationship." I open my mouth to speak but he cuts me off as his eyes open and he looks at me with pleading eyes. "I know we have things to talk about and decisions to make but just for tonight, I want to enjoy *us* and not think about everything else. Please?"

"OK." I say and I force myself to relax as I run my fingers through the hair on his chest. There isn't a lot but I love playing with it. I know there are women that love a smooth, naked chest, just like there are men out there like a hairless pussy but I love men with hair on their chest. It soothes me in a way that I don't understand and don't want to delve in to too much.

We spend the next few minutes talking until my answers are only mumbles and I feel his chest rumble with laughter.

"Sleep gorgeous. You're gonna need it." He kisses the top of my head lightly and that's the last thing I remember until I'm woken up by the low rumble of his voice in the distance and the scent of pizza wafting into the room.

I force myself to wake up properly and sit up in bed. I need a couple of minutes before I swing my legs over the side and start to find some clothes to put on. Just as I finish pulling on some leggings and a t-shirt, Matt walks up to the door and leans against the doorframe, legs crossed at the ankle and one arm leaning against the doorframe. He looks so sexy with the light from the other room behind him and I have to stop myself from jumping on him and going for another round.

"I was just coming in to wake you up. I ordered pizza, I hope that's OK?" I can just make out the sweet smile on his face. The man doesn't lack confidence but he is aware that he pushes my limits of control sometimes.

"Of course!" I say a little too chirpily. "I woke up because I could smell it. Did you get me a-."

"Chicken pizza with pineapple." He shakes his head and takes my hands in his to lead me out of the bedroom. "You my love, are a disgrace! Pineapple does *not* belong on pizza, ever!"

"I beg to differ." I answer with a shrug of my shoulders. We argue about this every time we get pizza and I doubt either of us are going to change how we feel about it.

"You're lucky you're cute." He tells me as he kisses the tip of my nose.

"You're lucky you're sexy." I say, stretching up on my tiptoes and kissing his cheek. I love this feeling of domesticity with him, even though in a small corner of my conscience it scares the hell out of me.

Chapter Four
MATT

After an hour of lying in bed with Sara snuggled up to me, I decided to get out and let her sleep for a while. I knew I wasn't going to sleep but she obviously needed the rest, so I got up and cleaned up the kitchen and living room for her, had a really quick shower and then ordered pizzas.

I figured I should have woken her up *before* the pizzas arrived but she looked so adorable while she slept, I couldn't bring myself to do it, even when I knew it would take her at least ten minutes to wake up enough to eat, I still couldn't do it. I was surprised to find her throwing on some clothes when I did go to wake her, I should have known she'd be able to smell food before I opened the door.

Don't think I didn't notice the fact that she skipped right past me calling her *my love* while we argued about pineapple not belonging on pizza too. She's become quite the expert at dodging terms of affection and not just the ones I say to her but the ones that she *doesn't* call me as well!

I'm a patient man, I can wait until she's comfortable using any kind of term of affection and I know the first step to getting her to use one is getting her to accept that Leila, my sister and her best friend, won't be upset about our relationship. At least after the initial shock wore off anyway.

"What are you thinking so hard about?" Sara asks, taking another bite of that abomination of a pizza.

"What makes you think I'm thinking about anything, especially *hard?*"

"Because when you're thinking hard about something or you're worried, you get this cute little frown that creates *the* most adorable crease on the bridge of your nose, between your eyebrows." She runs her forefinger right over the very spot she's describing but on her face, causing me to frown even more. "Yup, just like *that.*" She declares, pointing at me. I know we spend plenty of time together and not all of it is in the bedroom or having sex for that matter but I didn't realise that she'd taken that much notice.

"Thanks for noticing." I smile at her but she dismisses me with a wave of her hand like anybody would have noticed something like that, even though we both know that's not necessarily the truth.

"Anyone would. What were you thinking so deeply about?"

"Why any normal human being would have pineapple on pizza." I tell her without hesitation. What? It's not like I can tell her the damned truth, that I'm in love with her and that I notice every time she skips around my terms of affection. I can't tell her that a little piece of my heart shatters every time she does it either. "It's an abomination, seriously, Sara." I tell her while shaking my head solemnly.

"What a load of shit!" She exclaims and I know I've distracted her from what I was really thinking about. "If you don't like pineapple on pizza, then don't eat it but you can't tell me that *I* can't like it. I don't eat food just because other people like it, especially if I can't stomach it." It's on the tip of my tongue to ask her if that's true of Leila but I catch myself in time so that I *don't* bring up my sister.

"Says the woman who cooks food for others for a *living*! What would you tell someone who wanted to change one of your recipes? You know the type, they order the salad but with lettuce on the side." She rolls her eyes and throws the crust of the slice she just finished eating on to the lid of the box.

"*No-one* orders salad *without* the lettuce and you know it! *If* they did, then that's what we would serve because that's their choice and it's *my* choice to have pineapple on my chicken pizza and you won't change my mind any time soon, no matter what argument you use."

"If you stop having pineapple on your pizza, I promise to do that thing you like every time we're together." I promise with a waggle of my eyes.

"You mean shut up and let me breathe in peace?" She asks, crossing her arms over chest and looking like she's pouting but I can see her fighting a smile.

"That too, gorgeous, that too." I drop my closed pizza box on the coffee table and take hers out of her hands, dropping it on top of my discarded pizza.

"Hey, I was eating that!" But her protest dies on her lips as I slide my lips along her jaw until I reach her ear, where I whisper my promise.

"I promise to eat you out every time we see each other if you can stop having pineapple on your pizza."

"Wh-what?" She stutters, as her eyes flutter closed.

"I. Promise. To. Lick. Your. Pussy. Every. Time. I. See. You."

"If – if I don't have pineapple. On my pizza?"

"For every time you don't have pineapple on your pizza, no matter who we're with, I promise to write the alphabet on your clit with my tongue until you come."

"You know, that-."

"Yeah, I know, so I think I might have to add the use of my fingers in your pussy too."

"Hmmmmm." She moans as her head rests on the back of the chair and I lick up her exposed throat.

"I'll hook my fingers and use that 'come hither' motion you love so much to reach that spot you like. You know, the one that makes you squirt all over my hand."

"Mmmm Hmmmm. Fuck Matt."

"Are you hot? Are you ready for me gorgeous?"

"Yes. Oh god yes!" She truly does look gorgeous. Legs spread, giving me easy access to her pussy if that's what I want. Her neck stretched so that I can lick, kiss and nibble her flesh. Eyes closed and a look of pure, unadulterated pleasure on her face.

I am *so* tempted to rip the body hugging leggings right off her body but I don't because that would be too easy, for the both of us.

"You'd like that, wouldn't you?"

"Yesssssss." I take those soft pouty lips with mine and I kiss her deeply, soundly, so that she knows she's been kissed and then I pull back. "What the?"

I pick up both of the pizza boxes and quickly deposit them in the fridge for tomorrow. Her eyes glisten in the overhead light of the living room and I know what she's expecting and I know exactly what she's *not* getting.

"So, I guess I'll see you tomorrow?" I ask, as I pick up my keys, phone and wallet that I left on the kitchen bench.

"Wh-what?"

"Well, we've hooked up, had something to eat and now it's time for me to leave. Right?" I ask innocently because for a long time in the beginning of whatever the hell this is, that's exactly what happened and I know it's because she didn't want me around to remind her of what she was doing.

"*Matthew.*" My name is more growl than an actual word and my already hard cock gets harder and more uncomfortable but I'm not going to adjust myself while she's watching. I know she can see my erection and I don't care!

"*Sara.*" I respond with my own growl.

"You can't leave me like *this*!"

"Like what, gorgeous?"

"You know what!"

"I do." I stalk back over to her and her eyes widen in surprise and then heat with desire. "Do you want to know what else I know?" She nods and I'm beyond happy that she can't speak in this moment. "I know you won't play with yourself when I leave. I *know* that you won't masturbate and do you know how I know that? I know that because I'm telling you, you can't and if you disobey me tonight, I will spend tomorrow night and the night after bringing you to the edge of your orgasm but I won't let you come. If you make yourself come tonight without me, I promise you that you're going to be *so* highly strung for the next few days, nothing but *me* is going to help you."

I pull away from her and walk to the door before she catches her breath and can speak.

"You can't tell me what to do, Matthew." She calls after me as I reach for the door handle.

"I believe I just did gorgeous." I tell her without looking back at her. "I also know that you believe what I'm telling you. You *know* that if you give herself relief tonight, you're going to be paying for it for the next two days. That's the risk you take."

I don't wait for her reply, she knows the rules and we both know she enjoys it. The promise and the edging. Before stepping off her back porch, I adjust my cock in my pants so that I can actually walk without looking like I've got a pole stuck up my arse and make my way to my car.

I'm going to need a shower when I get home and lucky for me, I don't have to make it a cold one because I'm not the one who can't take matters into their own hands tonight without punishment.

I drive all the way home with a huge smile on face, which only gets bigger when I receive a message as I pull into my driveway.

Sara: *You fucking bastard!*

Me: *You're welcome gorgeous*

I add a heart emoji because I know how she just loves it when I add emoji's to all our messages. Then, I crack up laughing because I can imagine the string of words that are leaving her mouth right now and all the names she's currently calling me.

That shower is looking really good right now and even though I had a quick shower at Sara's, I still make a beeline straight for my bathroom and my shower. Jerking off feels even better knowing that Sara's *not* doing the same thing.

I collapse into bed with a smile on my face. I really hope she can't resist making herself come tonight or tomorrow because I'm really looking forward to teasing her some more.

Chapter Five
SARA

The door slams shut behind him and my clit is buzzing so much I would think that I'd had a vibrator pressed against it and not a man a few seconds ago. Damn the man that left me with a very severe case of blue bean and *then* telling me, no *demanding* that I don't play with myself! Who does he think he is?

I scream into the quiet of my apartment, smothering my face with a pillow so a neighbour doesn't call the cops. When I'm done, I throw it aside and slide my hand down my stomach in defiance. Matthew fucking Phillips can't tell me what I can and can't do with or to my body. He'll never know if I do, I mutter into the quiet, as I run my hand down my stomach but I hesitate when I touch my bellybutton. He couldn't possibly tell if I rub one out tonight, it's not like he's watching me. I look around the room, checking for cameras and feeling like a complete fucking idiot. I roll my eyes and push my hand down a little further and just as my finger tip touches my clit, I stop again and not because my clit is so sensitive it's tingling, even though it is. No, I know, I just *know* he's going to know. Damn him!

Now, it's my choice as to whether I get relief now and pay the price tomorrow or wait. Either way, I'm pissed at him because I know that I'll enjoy my punishment and waiting.

"Fuck you, Matthew!" I scream, this time I don't bother with the pillow and a neighbour yells back something along the lines of shut the hell up. I flip them the bird even though they obviously can't see me, it makes me feel better and then I look for my phone.

I find it in the first place I look for it, on my bedside drawers. Matt must have put it there because I'm pretty sure I dropped it on the bed when he arrived earlier. Before can start to feel anything other than annoyed, I send him a message and almost immediately get one back.

Me: *You fucking bastard!*

Matt: *You're welcome gorgeous*

He adds a stupid fucking smiling emoji onto the end and I can hear him chuckling from here, which does nothing to dull my annoyance. At a guess, that's all part of his plan, so that I'll defy him and then he can do whatever he likes to punish me tomorrow. He should know better than that! Determined to not give into my body's desires but warring with myself about giving in to a man's demands about what I can or cannot do with my body is exhausting!

I decide having a shower is the best idea and then I'm going to bed. If I'm asleep I can't make a choice, right? I strip off in the bathroom, leaving my clothes in a pile on the floor and step into the shower. As I soap up my body, I can't help smiling. *Washing* myself can't be considered getting myself off, can it? Happy that I think I've found a loophole, I realise that even then, he's going to know because I'm going to be more relaxed tomorrow and not ready to jump his bones. I rinse my body, towel off and then walk to my bed, leaving everything else in a damp pile on the floor of the bathroom.

I drop into my bed, pull the covers over me and I can feel myself falling asleep. I'm right on that weird edge of not quite knowing if I'm awake or asleep when I hear my phone ringing but I can't tell if it's real or not and I don't have the energy to look, so I let it go. I can check it in the morning, I'm too tired tonight to care.

THE NEXT MORNING I wake up smiling, despite my alarm blaring from my phone because my dream was amazing. It's a dream that I'm not ready to wake up from because the thought of waking up with Matt's head between my legs is something I could get on board with.

I stretch and reach for my phone all in one movement but I can't move my bottom half and for a few seconds I panic. Then I hear his deep, rumbling voice and I relax for a second.

"It's just me."

"It's not a dream?" It's more a question than a statement and I feel the puff of his breath from his laughter on my pussy.

"No, Gorgeous, it is not. Now, turn off that racket so that I can concentrate on your pussy." His lips are resting against me and I can feel the vibration of his voice as it rumbles over my skin.

"What are you doing?" My words get cut off, my breath hitching as he swipes his tongue through my pussy, to press on my clit and I can't form the rest of my question.

"I'm licking your pussy." I can feel his smile against me.

"Smart arse!" I grumble and squeeze his head with my thighs, he chuckles because we both know I'm not holding him still, he's choosing to be *held*. "I meant, what the hell are you doing in here? I told you last night, I didn't give you that key so that you can waltz in and out of here any time you like. I might have had company."

That last sentence does exactly what I intended it to do. It pisses him off. He growls as he pushes my legs apart with force, slamming my knees into the mattress and prowling up my body, until he's nose to nose with me, his brown eyes flashing with anger.

"Who the hell else would you have here, between your legs, Sara?" For all my bravado I wonder what the hell I just did but I don't back down, it's just not in me.

"I didn't realise we were exclusive." I say but even I can hear the slight tremor in my voice.

"Yes, you did." He pulls back slightly so that he can really look into my eyes, reading in them everything I'm not saying out loud and it scares the shit out of me. "For the record, I haven't been with anyone else since we started seeing each other." He confirms what I suspected, what I dared to hope.

"We're not dating, Matt." Even to me that sounds like a lie, my voice isn't strong, there's no conviction in it and we both know.

"Tell me, Sara." I raise an eyebrow at him. "Tell me now or I'm leaving and I promise, I won't come back." I know what he wants me to tell him and even though I don't want him to leave, I can't bring myself to say it.

He rears up, throwing the covers off both of us and that's when I realise he's naked as well. How the hell did I sleep through him getting into my apartment, stripping off *and* crawling into bed with me? I'm scared for my own safety more than anything else. That is until I realise he's actually off the bed and putting his clothes back on.

"You're leaving?" I ask, dumbfounded. It's a stupid question, I can *see* him preparing to leave.

"I told you, if you couldn't tell me what I wanted then I was leaving, so yes." He's so matter of fact and he doesn't look at me when he speaks, he in fact, turns his back to me and picks up his shirt.

"Matt." I say his name quietly but I know he heard me but he doesn't stop getting dressed. "Matt." I say his name louder but he stays silent and keeps putting his clothes back on. I sit and move towards the end of the bed where he's standing and reach out to him. He steps just out of my reach and I sigh, realising that I've hurt him. "Matthew." I start to speak and his hands freeze on his belt.

"No." He says, his voice cold. "I'm done with this shit, Sara. Done." He doesn't move to keep getting dressed but neither does he move to look at me either.

"Matt, I'm sorry. Truly, I didn't think."

"You never do, Sara and that's the problem. It's always been about what you want, what you need. Well, guess what? I *thought* we were *something*. Something worth fighting for. I *thought* we were together and the reason you were so against telling my sister is because you were protecting me, us. But I was wrong, wasn't I? I was just another fuck toy. Something to pass your time with. Well, you can find someone else now because I am officially done, Sara."

"No!" That one word is so loud, I'm surprised my neighbour isn't banging on the wall. "It's not true! You're not a fuck toy, I've never had one of whatever that is." I shake my head trying to understand where things went wrong. I woke up to his head between my legs and now he's mad at me. "Please, don't go. Stay."

"I can't."

"You can, you're choosing not to." Now it's my turn to be pissed off again.

"No, I can't, Leila just messaged me and she wants to see me."

"Oh." The reminder that Leila is his sister definitely pours cold water over this conversation that's for sure. "Matt, I'm sorry."

"For what, Sara?" Finally, he turns around to look at me and I almost wish he hadn't because then I wouldn't be able to see the hurt and sadness in his eyes.

"I haven't been with anyone since we got together either." I take a deep breath. "I hadn't been with anyone before that for just over a year and you're the only guy I've slept with since. I wouldn't do that, Matthew, I wouldn't be with someone else if you didn't know about it. If that wasn't part of our agreement. I'm not a cheater and I wouldn't cheat on *you*." I want to add because I like him too much, that I need him more than I've ever needed anyone before him.

"I didn't call you a cheater."

"Didn't you?" I raise an eyebrow at him. "Because you kind of did just by not letting me tell you the truth, by jumping to conclusions. This is one of the reasons I think the age gap is too much, Matt. You go off half-cocked and assuming without talking to me."

"It's not like you're talking either, Sara." He's right, I know he is but we're not talking about me right now.

"You're so."

"Don't say it." He warns.

"Young. You're just so damned young Matt and I want you to be sure. I *need* you to be sure that this is what you want, that *I'm* what you want because being with you, there are things that will change drastically in my life." I hold my hand up to stop him from talking when his mouth opens. "You asked, so I'm explaining." I sigh. "I'm not going to lie, when we first hooked up I was thinking that this would be just that, a hook up, a fling but it wasn't, it became something else. Something I wasn't expecting and I'm not complaining, not at all but you came from nowhere, Matt."

"Something good? Something worthwhile?" He looks every one of his years, so much younger than me and it hurts.

"I don't know. Yes, yes!" I hurry on. "But that doesn't mean I'm ready to tell the world and that's not because it's you and it's not because Leila is your sister. I need to know that we're good, that we're strong enough to withstand it, Matt because if I lose my job and my best friend, I'm going to need to know that I still have *you* and I know this might hurt your feelings but right now, I don't feel like we could. We're all about the sex, which is great, amazing really, but that doesn't make for a real, stable relationship. I've been there, done that and don't want to do it again *but* I understand that you're young, that this probably *does* feel like the real deal to you and I don't want to tell you that it isn't."

"But you're telling me it isn't, right?"

"I don't know, Matthew. I really don't and that's why I don't want to tell everyone just yet." I see the hurt cross his face and I know, this *discussion* is far from over.

Chapter Six
MATT

"Yet? It's been *six months,* Sara!" I know I sound pathetic and I'm probably proving to her that I'm young, stupid and impulsive but I don't care. "Six months isn't nothing."

"I know but it's not *something,* either." She says quietly and it's like a slap in the face.

"You're right, it's not." I nod and keep getting dressed. "I'll leave the key on the bench."

"Matt. No!" I walk out of her bedroom as fast as I can manage, while feeling like a new born deer trying to find their legs. "If you walk out that door -." I don't let her finish, I look back her and she's standing in her doorway, naked except for a t-shirt she's managed to find to cover her front. It's hard not to walk over to her, take her in my arms and kiss her until neither of us can breathe properly but I'm not doing this anymore.

"Or what Sara? Hmmm? You'll kick me out? I'm already leaving. You'll break up with me? That's already done, honey. I'm leaving and I'm not coming back. You think I'm too young? You think this isn't enough? I disagree but I'm not going to be your doormat anymore either." I slam the key on the bench and storm to the front door. My hand rests on the handle and I take a deep breath before saying, "Goodbye Sara. Have a great life. Oh and hey, if you see me at Vines, don't say hello. That's the way you like it, right?" I open the door and slam it behind me as I leave.

The loud slamming of the door makes me smile but my satisfaction is short lived when I realise what I've actually done. I may not have wanted to end things with Sara, I *know* I fell in love with her weeks ago but I won't be walking back into her apartment to beg her to take me back either. She might like to think that I'm too young and immature and that perhaps my behaviour just now proves it but I know I'm looking out for myself.

I get in my car, slam that door shut as well, message my sister to let her know I'll be there in half an hour and start the car. When I look up, I see a now dressed Sara standing in the open doorway of her apartment building. I guess I should be grateful that she followed me but I'm pretty sure she has to get to work today and that means I'm not the reason she's in the carpark.

I stare at her for a second, waiting, *hoping* that she'll come to me, ask me to give her, *us,* another chance but she's frozen to the spot. So, I gun it out of my parking space and don't look back. Well, I don't look in the rearview mirror more than twice because the second time I can barely make out whether that's her still standing in the doorway.

It's not until I reach the gates to Drake Wines that I realise that I've driven here completely on auto pilot. I have no actual memory of driving here and that scares the hell out of me. As I pull up beside Vines, I shake my head to clear it and turn off the car. I have get my shit together before I go in there and talk to my sister. She'll know within seconds that something is wrong and I won't get away from her without answering a million and one questions that I simply don't have the answers to. Well, not the answers that she wants to hear or that I want to tell her, for that matter.

When I look up, I see Leila standing at an empty table watching me, her head cocked to one side and an eyebrow raised.

Fuck! She already knows there's something wrong and we haven't even spoken yet.

Sighing, while bracing myself for the inevitable, I get my sorry arse out of the car and make my way inside. Which is when I realise with horror that Leila is going to expect not only a hug but a kiss on the cheek. As if on cue, she's right in front of me, arms outstretched, ready to embrace me and I try hard not to flinch.

"Sorry Sis, I need to go to the bathroom. Can our hug wait until after? I'm ready to explode!" I say, dodging around her and rushing towards the bathroom.

"Are you still twelve Matthew? Can't you survive a thirty minute car ride without a trip to the bathroom?" She's teasing me but it's still hurts just a little.

"Too much coffee already this morning Lei." I call out as I burst into the Men's room. I lean over the basin and start splashing water all over my face. When I'm done, I lean on the sink and look up into to the mirror. When my eyes meet mine in my reflection, I start laughing. To anyone else, I know I'd look and sound crazy, insane probably but I know I need to get this out.

What would Leila have said if she'd known that the last place my face had been was between her best friend's legs? That the last thing *my* lips had touched before giving *my sister* a kiss, was the lips of her best friend's pussy! I couldn't do it. I wouldn't have been able to kiss my sister no matter whose pussy juices I'd had on my face but the fact that I had Sara all over my lips and chin? Not such a great idea I would say.

"Hey, are you OK Matty?" Leila's voice is muffled from the other side of the closed door and I've never been more grateful to come visit her at work because if we'd been at her house or mine, she would have just barged into the bathroom. Here she can't simply because it's her workplace and the men's room.

"Yeah, I'm good, Lei. I'll be out in a second. Why don't you order me a coffee and whatever delicious cake you've got going on today?" There's a pause and I sigh because I know she hasn't left. "Please? Thank you, Lei."

"If you're sure?" She doesn't sound convinced and I know I'm going to have my work cut out for me today.

"Absolutely." I can't hear if she moves away but I'm assuming she has because she's not asking me any more questions.

I look at myself in the mirror and chuckle once more. I'm a fucking mess! I've got water dripping down my face and my beard is a shambles as well. Luckily for me, the Drakes have both an air hand dryer and paper towels. So, I grab some paper towel and dry my face, then use the air dryer to dry my beard a bit, using my fingers to comb it into a neater version of itself.

Smiling into the mirror, I straighten myself up and leave the bathroom, only to come face to face with my sister!

"What's going on, Matt?"

"Nothing, I was hoping breakfast might be on the cards though?" I smile at her, hoping I can convince her that all is good with me.

"You want cake for breakfast?" She raises an eyebrow at me. "I won't feed your sugar addiction Matthew, you need something more filling first thing in the morning." I flinch at her using my full name because it reminds me of Sara and I don't need that right now.

"Great plan. How about we start on that tomorrow and today, I get cake?" Her arms are crossed over her chest and she's looking at me like she knows what I'm thinking. "Lei, just for today, can you just be my friend and not my big sister, please? Today I need a coffee strong enough that a spoon could stand up unaided in it and some cake, OK? And yes, everything *will* be OK, I just need *this today*." I drop a kiss on her forehead. "And for the love of all that's holy, can we move the fuck away from the bathrooms, please?" I ask laughing, putting my hands on her shoulders and turning her around and walking her back to the dining room.

"Good morning, Leila, Matthew." Georgie says, a warm smile on her face.

"Morning, Georgie. How are you?" I've always liked the barista at Vines. She's beautiful inside and out, plus she's smarter than anyone else I know.

"I'm good, Matthew. Are you OK?" A frown mars her beautiful face and I almost regret coming here this morning. Perhaps I should have told Leila I was busy and just headed straight home?

"I'm perfectly fine, thanks for asking beautiful." I say with a wink and turn on my heels, only to be faced with a different frowning woman. The one I just left in her apartment after telling her we're done. "Nothing a strong coffee and a slice of your delicious chocolate cake won't fix."

"Coming right up, Matthew." Georgie says from behind me. She sounds distant to me but that's only because every fibre of my being has zoned in on Sara, she's like a siren to my body and I can't help reacting to seeing her here. Here, where I knew she'd be eventually.

"Good morning." I nod at Sara, without waiting for her reply, I talk to Leila. "I'll go grab us a table." Before she can say anything, I walk away to find us a table that is away from the occupied ones because I know there are questions coming.

I'm only left to stare out the window at the gorgeous vineyard beyond for a few minutes before my sister sits herself down in the chair opposite me. I resist taking my eyes off the view because I'm afraid of what she might find if she looks in my eyes. My big sister has always had this incredible knack of being able to read my mind and it's annoying as fuck sometimes.

"Are you sure you're OK, Matt? You were pretty rude to Sara back there." I close my eyes for a second, before tearing my eyes away from looking out the window, to look at my sister, a smile firmly fixed on my lips.

"Absolutely. I'm sorry, I didn't meant to be rude, I was just saying hello."

"Are you sure?"

"Yes! Now, can we stop with all the questioning about how I'm feeling, please?" My smile feels more like a grimace now.

"If that's what you want, Matt but it's just that I worry about you, you know?" I did know.

"I know Lei but I promise, I'm OK." I sigh and decide to tell a small fraction of the truth. "If you want the truth, a girl I was seeing broke things off with me. I guess I just wasn't enough for her." I say, just as Georgie arrives with breakfast.

"What woman in her right mind would think you're not good enough for her? The woman must be mad!" Georgie says with a shake of her head. If only she knew!

"Thanks Georgie, I appreciate the vote of confidence but we can't help the way other people think or feel. If she says I'm not the right person for her, then I have to trust that she's right." I say with a smile that I know won't look like I mean it but it's all I can manage.

"Well, you're being very generous and kind. Another reason I think this woman is nuts but you're right, if she not feeling it, then that's her loss." She bends down and pecks my cheek, while giving me an awkward one armed hug with the empty tray in her hand.

"Thanks beautiful but it is what it is, I guess." I shrug. Georgie walks away after giving me one last sympathetic smile.

"OK, I'll ask one more time. Are you *sure* you're OK?" Leila asks, concern written all over her face.

"Honestly?" She nods her head as she takes her first tentative sip of her coffee. "I'm feeling a little wounded right now but I'll be OK. I promise."

"Were you seeing her for long?"

"Long enough that I thought it was leading to something but she had other ideas."

"Oh, Matty, I'm sorry." Leila reaches over and pats my hand with hers and I feel like a little boy again. "Georgie's right, the woman is crazy if she thinks you're not good enough for her." I snort out a laugh, if only she knew!

"I don't want to be with someone who thinks I'm not enough." I smile sadly at my sister. "That's enough about me, I don't want to be sad, it happened and it's over. What are we talking about here today?"

"I wanted to talk to you about Mum and her 'friend'."

"Oh, so you found out about Jack then?" I ask.

"You knew?"

"I found out accidentally when I went to visit unannounced." I shudder. "Let me tell you, I've learned that lesson, I'm never not calling Mum again before I visit. I suggest you do the same thing unless you want to bleach your eyeballs."

"No?!" Leila gasps.

"Oh yes, my dear sister. I took that hit for you and you're welcome but I'm not planning on another one." I laugh at the look of disgust on her face and then lose it all together when she shudders and dry retches.

I dig into my cake and drink my coffee, as Leila tells me all about her call with our mum and we talk about all kinds of things that make us both laugh and shudder.

The whole time I can feel Sara's eyes on me but I never turn to look at her, not once. I can't because I know if I do, I'll break and kiss her, then chaos will ensue, causing more problems than I can deal with today.

So, I don't turn around, I keep my focus on my sister.

Chapter Seven

SARA

Call me crazy but I didn't think he was actually *serious* when he told me not to talk to him if I saw him at Vines!

I can't help watching from the small port window in the kitchen, as he talks and laughs with Leila, ignoring my existence and flirting with Georgie.

When I walked in to start my shift not much longer after he would have arrived himself, he was already seated and relaxing with his sister. I happened to walk in just as he and Georgie were flirting and wasn't that joyful? Not! I know I behaved like an idiot and gave Georgie a dirty look.

Leila said good morning and laughed when I grumbled my good morning in return, accusing me of not seeing the guys I've told her vaguely about and therefore, I was obviously 'a little highly strung'. What she meant to say was that I was left hanging, high and dry without an orgasm.

She wasn't wrong.

The entire time I spoke to his sister, Matt ignored me.

I've known him almost since the day I met Leila. He was here a lot in the beginning and then disappeared for a while. We met up in the city one day and well, the rest I guess you could say, is history. We got along and got together.

That was six months ago.

Every time he comes into Vines, we struggle to be normal around one another. I have no fucking clue how no-one around us has noticed but they haven't. Not that they've mentioned anything to me anyway.

"Sara." I hear my name but ignore it. I'm thinking about all the time we wasted, that I wasted, not telling Leila about us and staring out that tiny damned window at Matt. "Sara."

"What?" I almost scream at the person who is calling my name as I turn to face them.

"What's the matter?" I turn to find Leila's face staring back at me, concern written all over her face.

"Shit! Sorry, I didn't mean to yell at you. I was just concentrating on-." I look down at my hands to work out what the hell it is I'm actually doing, only to realise that, unfortunately, the dough I was kneading is no longer usable. "Fuck!" I mumble.

"Sara." Leila's hand rests on top of my mine lightly and even then, I still jump at her touch. "What's wrong?"

"Nothing. I'm sorry, OK? I was off on another planet, not really thinking about anything and got carried away." I lie. "I'll toss this in the rubbish and start again. Sorry about the waste of time and ingredients."

"Sara." I pull my hand out from under hers and walk over to the rubbish, dumping the ruined dough into it. "Sara, I'm not worried about the time or the dough. I'm worried about my friend. This isn't like you. Normally you could make that dough in your sleep, with your eyes shut and one hand tied behind your back. The fact that you screwed it up tells me everything I need to know."

"Oh yeah and what's that Leila? Hmmmm?" I know I'm being a bitch. *She* knows I'm being a bitch. We *both* know that's how I deflect and protect myself. Go on the defensive and don't let the bastards in or win. That way, they can't hurt me or break my heart.

Fuck me! It's what I did with Matt! I've been doing it with Matt this entire time. Keeping him at arm's length, so that he can't get close enough to hurt me. How, *why*, did it take me this long to work this out? I know myself pretty well, I know my faults and I know what I do to protect myself from emotional pain. Physical pain is something I can deal with easily, that shit heals. It's emotional scars, the ones that others can't see, that take time to heal and hurt the most.

"Sara." Leila's sweet voice brings me back to the present and I feel guilty for spacing out on her once again. "What happened?"

"He dumped me." I admit, surprising myself. Even more surprising is the fact that I can feel the tears welling in my eyes, ready and waiting to fall down my cheeks. I'm not a crier. I learned early in life that tears didn't do shit to help in a situation, in fact, they normally made it a hell of a lot worse. "Shit." I say, swiping at the *one* tear that dares to drop to the apple of my cheek. "Sorry, I'll get right back to work and I promise, there won't be any injuries today because I'm not concentrating on what I'm doing." I give her a weak and watery smile and turn away from her, before the sympathy on her face makes me bawl like a baby. Imagine if she knew that I was crying over her *brother*! She wouldn't be feeling quite so empathetic then I imagine.

"Ohhh, Sara, I'm so damned sorry. I know you liked this guy." She says and before I can react, she wrapping her arms around my waist from behind me, resting her cheek on my back.

"How would you know how much I liked him?" I ask, curious and trying to work how to get my stupid arse out of this weird situation I've found myself in. "I haven't even told you his name, Leila." I know she's smiling because I felt the movement of her cheek on my back.

"That's one of the reasons I know you like him, Sara, you're keeping him close to your chest. Savouring him." God, if *only* she knew the *truth*! "Another one is the way your face lit up when you spoke about him." It did? "I could always tell when you'd seen him because you'd walk in here happy, smiling and almost cheerful." She laughs because she feels the shudder that runs through my body at the mere mention of me being *cheerful*.

"You were seeing someone?" A deep voice asks from the doorway and I know who it belongs and I don't want to see him. Leila steps away from me and I feel the loss of her embrace immediately but I don't turn around to look at the siblings as they continue to talk. About me.

"Yes, she was and while I can't tell you much about him, she did seem to be very taken with him. She was almost dreamy when she spoke about him." Leila laughs, not knowing that she's killing me and giving her brother more reasons to walk away. "Sara doesn't get dreamy about guys but this one, he seemed different."

"Maybe you could talk, maybe work it out?" Matt says from the doorway and I can feel his eyes boring into the back of my head but I don't turn around to face them. I can't.

"I doubt that. The decision was made and he was pretty clear that his decision was final. No compromise."

"Nothing is ever a done deal until you both agree, Sara." Leila declares. "Maybe he can be reasoned with?"

"Maybe Lei's right, maybe you could talk to this guy. Explain it all to him. Tell him how you really feel about him. You never know, he might come around." Matt suggests. The gall of him to suggest *more* talking when he *knows* what was said. I guess having his sister around to cover his gorgeous arse, he can say whatever the hell he wants?

"No, I think it's for the best. He's made up his mind. He's the one who walked away, not me and I won't chase him. He decided I wasn't enough, so while I'm hurt right now, I think it's better to just let it and him go. He'll be much happier and I can go on with my life."

"It's his loss sweetie. I mean, the guy must be a real moron to not realise how great you are. You're amazing, you know that right? And not just because you're almost as good at baking as I am but because you're one of my favourite people on the planet. Forget about this idiot, he doesn't know what he's talking about." Her mini rant makes me smile, if only she knew that she just called her brother an idiot *and* a moron right to his face without realising it.

"You shouldn't be back here." I say, loud enough for Matt to hear behind me.

"She's right you know." Leila agrees as she starts pushing her brother back out to the dining area. "I get that you were worried about Sara but you're going to have to stay out here for now. Get yourself another coffee, I'm sure Georgie won't mind helping you with that."

My stomach churns at Leila's innocent suggestion that her brother go talk and perhaps flirt, with Georgie but without turning around to look at them, I have no idea what his reaction to it is. What I *do* know is that I can hear their heated whispering just outside the door and I don't want to know what's being said, so I get to work making a new batch of the dough I just stuffed up.

"Sorry about Matt, I didn't even think about him being back here. He's my little brother, I'm just kind of used to him following me around everywhere." She chuckles and I guess it would be cute, if my heart wasn't breaking into a million little pieces after that conversation and then thinking about him talking to Georgie.

"You're really upset, aren't you Sara?" Leila asks and just that one simple question breaks me. I can't hold back the tears any longer and with a loud sob, I step back from the work bench, covering my face with my flour covered hands and I cry. I cry like I've never cried before. "Oh shit, Sara, I'm sorry."

"No, I'm sorry." I bark out between heaving sobs, while trying to catch my breath. "I don't do this, this isn't me." I say, as I lean against the wall and slide down to the floor. I know *why* I'm crying and feeling like an emotional wreck over him. I saw him in here, at Vines, not thirty minutes after he left me high and dry and dumped at my apartment. My emotions haven't had the chance to catch up and they're overwhelmed by the sadness that I can usually deal with on my own and then move on but this time it involves more than me and him. This time it involves her and every time I see Leila, my best fucking friend, I'm going to be reminded of *him*.

"Oh my god! Oh shit, Sara! I'm sorry, I didn't realise." Leila says, crouching down in front of me, taking my hands in hers.

"Didn't realise what?" I ask, innocently because I have no clue what she's realised all of a sudden.

"You're in love with him, aren't you?" There's a few seconds of silence before I admit it and then the room is filled with loud sobbing cries.

Chapter Eight
MATT

I know I shouldn't but knowing that I shouldn't doesn't stop me from standing on the other side of the door, listening to Leila and Sara talk. We *all* know that eavesdropping isn't a good idea, you rarely over hear the good things people say.

Today, I'm holding my breath as I listen to my sister and her best friend talk and when I hear a sob escape Sara, I'm tempted to bust back in there and hold her close. I want to make her feel better but I know better than to go barging back in there.

This is what Sara wants, she made her decision. She doesn't want my sister to know about us and I can't live that way anymore.

"You're in love with him, aren't you?" I hear my sister ask. There's a silence that I can't stand, I feel like I should walk away but I can't make my feet move. The silence seems to stretch out for an eternity before finally she answers Leila.

"Don't be ridiculous, Leila!" My heart sinks.

"Don't *you* be ridiculous, Sara. I can see it on your face. You don't cry over much and you certainly don't cry over a guy, none that I've seen anyway and yet here you are, crying over a guy who dumped you." I hear Leila sigh and Sara let out a quiet sob. "So, why don't you go with a bit of honesty, hmm? Honesty with yourself and me."

"You're one to talk!" Sara snorts and I tuck that away in my memory bank to ask my sister about later.

"We're not talking about me, Sara, I'm not the one standing in a corner of the kitchen, *at work,* crying into dough. Dough that you can make perfectly with your eyes shut and one hand tied behind your god damned back."

"Leila, don't, please." Sara begs, the pain in her voice cuts deep. "You don't understand and I can't explain it to you."

"You fell in love with him and then you pushed him away, didn't you?" There's another long fucking silence and I can picture quite clearly in my head what's going on behind that wall. My sister standing there, arms crossed over her chest and one foot tapping the ground, waiting out a pouting Sara who, for all the world, does not want to share one detail with her. "Sara?"

"Yes!" Sara's voice comes out thick with emotion and frustration. "Are you happy now? I fell in love with a man that I can't have, does that make you happy?" A crashing noise echoes out of the door and I let out the breath that I didn't even know I was holding. Well fuck!

"Of course that doesn't make me happy Sara! I want you to be happy, I want you to find love with a man that loves you just as much, if not more than you love him. You deserve to be happy." I hear a faint shuffling and then my sister's muffled voice speaks. "I'm sorry honey. Is he married or something, is that why you can't have him?"

"No! I wouldn't do that, well not on purpose, anyway."

"So, what happened?"

"It's complicated." I can barely hear Sara's mumbled answer.

"It can't be *that* complicated, Sara, nothing ever is."

"So, how about you and Caleb then? Is *that* complicated?" Sara's frustration making her lash out at my sister. "I'm sorry, Leila, I shouldn't have said that. I know that situation is complicated but trust me when I say, so is this one and if I could explain it to you, I would but I can't."

"Hey, Matt, have you got a table yet?" Georgie asks from behind me, making me jump. "Why are you just standing near the kitchen?" She laughs like this entire situation is hysterically funny.

"I was just-." I don't get to finish because Leila comes storming out of the kitchen.

"Because he was eavesdropping!" Leila answers for me. "Take him to a table as far away from the kitchen as you can get him please, Georgie." She turns to face me, a glare that could kill on her face. "You go sit down!" She points away from the doorway she's standing in and I see Sara peek around her.

"You and I are talking later." I stare at Sara and walk away before she can respond.

"You will leave Sara alone, Matthew, this doesn't concern you!" Leila says loudly enough for me to hear it. I flip her off and keep walking to a table, far away from the kitchen.

"Thank you, Georgie." I smile at her but I know it's not genuine and by the frown on her face, she knows it too.

"Is everything OK, Matt?" She places her hand on my shoulder and I want to shrug it off but I know it would be rude so I accept her touch begrudgingly.

"Yes, thank you, Georgie."

"I've never seen Leila that mad before." She turns to look back at the kitchen, giving me a chance to look over to catch Sara's eye. Only I can't because her eyes are fixed on where Georgie is touching me. Good! I can't help smiling and this time it *is* genuine. I know Sara sees it before Georgie turns back to face me because her frowns deepens.

"I can tell you didn't grow up with Leila as your big sister then, Georgie." I laugh and she joins me. "I'm glad she's usually a much friendlier boss than she can be as a big sister. Thank you for the drinks and food." I pat her on the hand that's still resting on my shoulder and it seems to bring her back to what she's supposed to be doing.

"I better get back to work. If there's anything you need, just yell out or come and get me." She smiles at me and pats my shoulder a couple of times before she walks away. I smile at her retreating back, I can *just* see Sara's reaction to what must appear to have been a cosy talk, out of the side of my vision and she's not happy.

I know that I'm not innocent, I could have easily asked Georgie to remove her hand but I didn't. I knew what I was doing but I also know that some people are touchy feely and Georgie has always been one of them. She doesn't mean anything by it and I'm in no way offended by it.

"Do you *have* to flirt with my staff?" Leila asks as she sits in the seat opposite me.

"*You* practically told me to!"

"I did no such thing, Matthew!" My sister says, aiming for shocked but I can see the glint in her eyes. "I would never tell you to flirt with any member of staff at *my workplace*!" Then, she scowls at me, that glint of mischief in her eyes replaced with a mixture of anger and a vague understanding of the situation.

"You kind of did, Leila and you know it. Now *why* you did, I'm not entirely sure but you did." I bring my coffee up to take a sip but it's still hot, so I rest my elbows on the table, cup of steaming coffee poised in front of me.

"I think I'm beginning to understand just fine, Matthew." Ohhh that raised eyebrow, and frown combo used to really intimidate me when we were kids but we're not kids anymore.

"You *think* you know what's going on, Leila but I'm not sure you truly understand the situation." I place my cup back on the table and stare down into it. I *want* to look over to the kitchen. I *want* to see if Sara's watching us, wondering if I'm telling my sister the truth about what's going on, about *us* but I don't. I don't look for a couple of reasons, one of which is because it will confirm what my sister thinks and because I know, without a doubt, that I won't stay seated at this table if I see Sara's face.

"Do *you* know who this guy is, Matthew?" Leila asks, her voice quiet and when I don't answer, she repeats the question. "Do you know who this guy is Sara's into, Matthew?"

"Why would I know who your best friend is or was, dating?" I ask, deflecting her question that I have no damned intention of answering.

"Are *you* the guy she was dating and fell in love with, Matthew?" The frown hasn't left her face and I can see her brain ticking over, thinking and wondering what the connection here is.

"Don't be crazy Leila, of course it's not me." I scoff and hope like hell that Sara can't hear me. Before Leila can continue her interrogation, a man I recognise as Caleb Drake appears.

"Hi, I'm Caleb." He holds his hand out for me to shake and the other one rest quite possessively on my sister's shoulder. My sister doesn't shake off the touch but leans into it, almost melting into it in fact.

"This is Matthew, my brother." I've met Caleb briefly a few times since Leila started here but apparently I'm either not memorable or I didn't matter too much previously. Not until he became quite possessive of my sister and who she spends time with anyway, which is *very* interesting.

"We've met a couple of times." I say as I stand up to take his hand in mine, making sure to place a little extra pressure into the hold. I watch as his smile widens and he shakes my hand until I let go. I think I might like this one.

"Of course! Sorry it's been a busy few weeks and my brain is slightly fried." Caleb's smile is easy and appears quite genuine.

"Are you here for your cake and coffee?" Leila smiles up at the man standing next to her like he hung the sun, the stars and the damned moon.

"I am, yes."

"I'll go tell Georgie." When she goes to stand up, Caleb gently pushes her back down with the hand that's still resting on her shoulder.

"I'll go do that, you stay here with your brother."

"Caleb."

"*Leila.*" He says her name in warning and she smiles at him! "I'm more than capable of ordering for myself, Darlin'." Leila blushes and I swear that's the first time I've ever seen her blush! "I'll talk to you later, after your visit with your brother."

"Why don't you join us?" I ask, hoping to take the heat off myself and onto these two.

"No, I can wait, it looks like you and your sister were in the middle of a serious discussion." Before he walks away, they look each other in the eyes and seem to have a conversation without words, then he nods and walks away. Georgie looks up and smiles at him, pointing to a table, where I see a steaming cup and a slice of cake already sitting there waiting for him.

"Geez! I take it the man is in here on a regular basis?"

"Every day, he works in here most days." Leila says a goofy smile on her face. "Stop distracting me. What's going on with you and Sara?"

"Nothing, Leila." I roll my eyes at her. "She's your best friend and colleague. I promised you I would never cross that line."

"You did make that promise but that was a long time ago Matt and you can't help who you fall in love with. Sometimes lines get blurred." She says quietly, almost wistfully.

I can't help wondering if she's still talking about Sara and myself or Caleb and herself. Either way, I have this strange feeling that my sister might understand the situation I've found myself in more than I ever thought. More than Sara gives her credit for.

Do I still think she'll be a little annoyed with us? Yes, mainly because we've kept it from her for so long. As I look up to find Caleb Drake watching my sister's every move, I have a funny feeling, it wouldn't turn out as badly as Sara has assumed it would.

Chapter Nine
SARA

I watch Leila and Matt chat away through the little porthole window that Leila loves watching Caleb work through, like they're chatting about the weather. It's annoying the shit out of me! I don't know how Matthew can sit out there, chatting away to his sister and pretend so easily and convincingly that I'm not here. Not to mention, he barely even acknowledged my existence when I walked in!

Movement in the dining room catches my attention and I notice that we suddenly have a crowd out there, so I make my out of the kitchen towards the commotion. I watch in fascination as Caleb walks up behind Leila, placing his hand on her lower back and I see her relax into his touch. Isn't that interesting? Caleb greets the older couple that have managed to spill some secrets to the entire bistro.

"Fiancé?" Logan's voice is quickly joined by both Matt's and Makenna's, all pretty much asking the same thing.

"So, you didn't know either?" Matt's facing away from me and asks the older Drake siblings, who both reply with a very resounding, "No!"

Both of them giving Brady, Makenna's husband a dirty look when he offers his congratulations to the apparently happily engaged couple.

"We're not. We haven't." Leila stutters out, then all hell breaks loose. People are talking over one another and wanting answers to questions. Poor Leila looks like a deer caught in the headlights of an oncoming truck.

"I knew it! I knew something was going on between the two of you!" I shout, catching everyone's attention, until Logan's voice booms out over all of the other voices and he takes command of the situation, directing everyone into the tasting room. He's not wrong when he suggests they should have this discussion in private.

"I'll stay out here and help Georgie." I tell Leila, stepping up to give her a tight hug. "But you and I? Yeah, we're talking once this mess is done, got it?" I smile at her because I know she's panicking right now but she doesn't have to worry about me or Vines.

When Betty, one of our regulars, comments that Logan doesn't have to take them all into the other room, he sends her one of his glares but she doesn't falter. She just smiles up at him and he storms away.

When I stepped back from Leila, I slammed into a solid body behind me and when that person touches me, I don't need to look behind me to know who it is. With his hands on my hips to steady me, Matt leans down and whispers in my ear, "We're talking after this too." Then he's joining the rest of the crowd walking into the tasting room.

I watch them all walk away and as the door closes behind them, Matt glances my way and I see everything I need to know in his eyes. He's not walking away as easily as I thought he would this morning.

"They could have stayed out here!" Betty complains, while her companions all agree whole heartedly, nodding so vigorously that I'm afraid their head might fall off.

"So, what's going on with you and Leila's brother?" Beryl asks.

"Young Matthew, isn't it?" Martha asks before I can answer.

"He's a handsome young man too. I wonder how he feels about older women?" Edith wonders out loud.

"You're too old for him Edith." Beryl admonishes her friend.

"An old woman can dream though." Edith pouts and I try not to laugh at their banter.

"Don't you have the hots for Caleb?" I ask with a smile.

"Oh no dear, that's Martha." Betty tells me and the lady in question pokes her tongue out at her friend.

"Don't think you can distract us from the original question young lady. We might be old but we still have all of our faculties."

"I'm well aware." I mumble, not wanting to offend them, they're *very* regular customers in Vines after all.

"We're not deaf either." Sarcasm dripping from each word as Martha rolls her eyes at me! These women, I'm telling you!

"You know, ladies, I want to be you when I grow up." I laugh.

"Which one?" Betty asks, a mischievous grin on her face that, quite frankly, makes me a little uncomfortable.

"*All* of you!" I tell them. "Now, how about a slice of Leila's famous chocolate cake and a fresh refill of your hot drinks. All on Vines, of course."

"You mean, Caleb's famous chocolate cake." Edith smirks.

"Sure, that one. How about four slices of Caleb's famous chocolate cake and new coffees?"

"Sounds fantastic." Betty agrees with a smile. I nod and walk back to where Georgie is already making up a new batch of hot drinks for our favourite table of granny's.

"Are you sure that was the right thing to do?" She asks me, nodding her head in their direction. "You know, they'll just get rowdier with more coffee in them."

"That's a chance I'm willing to take, if it takes the heat off Leila and Caleb for a while."

"Did you know about those two?"

"I wasn't sure but I'm not surprised, if that's what you're asking." I smile at her.

"And you and Leila's brother? What's going on there?" She nods towards the door to the tasting room and I look up just as Matt walks back into the dining room.

"I don't know." I tell her honestly. I don't give her the chance to respond, I pick up the four plates of cake topped with dollops of thick cream that would keep the biggest kid happy and take them to the table full of my favourite adult kids I know. "Here you go ladies." I place a plate down in front of each of them, successfully ignoring Matthew until the fine hairs on my arms stand to attention. I don't need to look around to know that he's right behind me. If I was even slightly unsure it was him, Betty lets me know I'm not wrong.

"Matthew, isn't? Leila's brother?" Betty asks. "I'm Betty and these are my friends, Edith, Martha and Beryl."

"It's nice to meet you ladies." He smiles that stupidly charming smile at each one of them, making them swoon in turn and I can't help it, I roll my eyes. He knows what he's doing because the hand that he's place lightly on my hip tightens. "I need to steal the beautiful Sara for a few minutes, if you ladies don't mind that is?" More smiling and Betty actually bats her eyes at him!

"We don't mind at all but you might want to take a bit longer than a few minutes young man. A lady likes a little bit of time spent on her, if you catch my meaning and I have no doubt whatsoever that Sara is one of those young ladies."

"Martha, cut it out!" I admonish her but they're all laughing. That is, until Matthew leans in like he's telling them a secret.

"You're right, she is and I love to give her as much time as she wants." He winks at them and gently nudges me towards a corner of the dining room that's empty. "Georgie. I just need to talk to Sara for a few minutes, we'll just be over there if you need anything." This time he sends that charming smile to Georgie and my insides bubble with jealousy.

I didn't even see Georgie walk up to the granny's table but there she is, placing fresh coffees in front of everyone and cleaning up their empty cups. It's not something I'm familiar with so it takes a second to realise what it is and she looks at me like she knows exactly what I'm thinking, so I frown at her.

"Come on, killer, let's talk." Matthew chuckles quietly in my ear and I let him lead me away from my customers and staff.

"Matthew, stop!" I demand as he walks me to a table in the corner but neither of us sit down. "I have a job to do Matthew and in case you haven't noticed, your sister is a little preoccupied with some Drake family business. Which means, I'm needed in the kitchen, Georgie isn't the only one who needs my help." I huff, turning to make my way back to the kitchen.

"They'll be fine for a few minutes, Sara. Georgie knows where you are and yes, I've noticed that Leila has a few things to deal with." He reaches out and lightly takes my upper arm in his hand to stop me from walking away. We both know, that if I really wanted to, I could break his hold and walk away but I don't. Instead, I turn around to face him, effectively breaking his hold on my arm as I do.

"Fine. Didn't you say everything you wanted to this morning?" I ask, still wounded by his words earlier. "Or do you have more salt to rub into the wounds you already opened?" I watch his face as he winces and I know he feels my anger, my hurt feelings but I'm not feeling very forgiving at the moment.

"I'm not going to lie to you and tell you that I didn't mean a word, I did and you know it. What I am going to apologise for is hurting you. That wasn't my intention but, and it's no excuse at all, I was hurting too."

"You had your feelings hurt, so you decided to lash out and hurt me? That seems like a very mature, grown up thing to do Matthew." I know I've hit home when I see the anger flare in his eyes. It shouldn't turn me on that he's passionate enough about *us* that I can bring him to anger so quickly but it fucking does. Any sign of emotion, good or bad, is better than apathy. Believe me, I've seen apathy and it is painful. To watch and be on the receiving end of. "Look, *Matt.*" I say, putting an emphasis on the shortened version of his name because I know he loves it when I call him by his full name. "I think you said everything you needed or wanted to earlier. I don't have anything else to say." I turn to walk away again and this time he doesn't reach out to stop me. Not physically, anyway.

"You may not have anything else to say but I do Sara Bankes and you're going to stay here and listen to me."

Chapter Ten
MATT

"Who the hell do you think you are?" Sara demands, as she spins around to shoot daggers my way. I watch the anger change to frustration and annoyance because she knows she's turned on when I command her to do things as well. Each one of those emotions flit across her gorgeous face and I know they're going to settle on anger. She's angry with me, for sure but she's even more so at herself. "This is my place of *work, Matthew.*" She hisses.

"I know, that's why I'm having this conversation in the corner of the shop that's empty, *Sara.*" I try to get the aggravation I'm feeling out of my voice but it's still there. "I want to talk to you."

"Why? You said and did everything you needed to earlier. What could have possibly changed?"

"You're right, I said a lot of things earlier."

"I know, I was there and I don't require a repeat, least of all *here.* Where I work and where *your* sister works. You know, the woman who just got herself into some kind of mess with the Drakes. I think that's more important than us because there *is* no us!"

"I'm not in any mess with the Drakes." Leila says from behind Sara, making her jump and her eyes widen as she spins around to look at my sister. "What do you mean, *us?* What's going on between you two?" She looks between us and before I can answer her, Sara does.

"Nothing. *Nothing* is going on between your brother and I. We were wondering if *you* were OK. He was filling me in on what happened with your little meeting back there." She nods towards the back room of Vines that honestly, before today, I didn't even know existed.

"Everything is fine." I walk over to Leila and pull her into my arms.

"Are you *sure* you're OK?" I ask. "I'm not interested in how anyone else is feeling, including Caleb, I want to know that *you're* OK."

"I'm fine. I promise." She mumbles into my chest, while squeezing me tight, then she pulls out of our embrace. "So, what's going on between you two then?"

"Nothing." Sara says a little too quickly. "Honestly Leila, your brother is just that, *your brother.* Your *younger* brother too might I add, you know how I feel about young guys."

"Ohh yes, I do but Matt isn't like the guys you like to pick on. He's smart and he's caring. You know what? I think you'd be lucky if my brother wanted to be with you, you could definitely do worse than him. He's a great catch, so if you wouldn't give him a chance just because of his age, that's your loss!"

"Thanks Lei." I say with a huge smile.

"You're welcome, Matt but I'm just being honest." She returns my smile for a few seconds and then it turns into a frown. "You're the guy who just dumped her, aren't you?"

"He's not." Sara says. "Why don't you go back and see if Caleb needs anything? I'm sure he could do with some moral support out there with Logan and Makenna, right?"

"How do you know it's just the three of them left out there?"

"I saw the rest of them rush out the side door and scoot to their houses like their arses were on fire!" Sara says, rolling her eyes. "They were like rats deserting a sinking ship honestly."

"He said he didn't need my help."

"Do you think he meant it? I mean, wouldn't *you* want moral support if you were facing those two about a new business prospect *and* your life all in one day. Within the same hour, actually."

"True." Leila looks at me and I can see her fighting with herself to stay with me or go to Caleb. "Will you be OK?"

"Of course! I'm a grown man, Leila. If I need anything, I'll ask Georgie." I smile at my sister and the amusement I see in her face tells me she knows. She knows why I said it and she thinks she knows how I feel about her best friend.

"And I'm sure, *Georgie* will be *more* than willing to help you out." She gives me one last hug and we both try not to laugh as we hear a low growl beside us. "I hope you know what you're doing." She says quietly in my ear letting me go. "I'm going to see if Caleb needs saving."

Sara starts to follow Leila until I take hold of her hand gently to stop her.

"Please, stay for a minute."

"No thanks, I'll send Georgie over to help you." She pulls out of my loose hold and I let her go. I know I hurt her this morning, I also know I can't make her talk to me or listen to me.

Instead, I sit down at the table and stare out the window, looking out over the vineyard. It's a beautiful property and the Drake sibling are lucky bastards living on it.

"Is everything OK?" I startle at Georgie's question.

"Hmmmm?" I look up at her, she's standing next to the table, a smile on her face that radiates happiness and a sense of calm.

"Are you OK? Why are you sitting over here in the corner staring out of the window?"

"I'm just waiting for Leila."

"Uhuh. I have a feeling she won't be back today." She looks out the window and smiles, I follow her gaze and see Leila, Caleb's arm around her waist, walking towards his house and I smile.

"I think you might be right, Georgie."

"Are you going to hang around anyway? I mean, she'll probably be over to close up."

"I'll stay for a while, yes." I smile at her but I know she can see that it's not as happy as usual. "Can I get a coffee and an apple cinnamon muffin please?"

"Sure. Did you want the muffin warmed up a little?"

"Yes, please."

"No worries, Matt." She touches my arm gently and her smile reflects my own feelings. "It will all work out, I promise."

"I'm sure Leila and Caleb will work everything out. They look pretty happy together." I look back out the window, towards Caleb's place and wonder for a second if I should go over there but decide against it.

"Oh, I know they'll be fine." She waves away my comment. " I wasn't talking about them, I was talking about you and Sara."

"There's nothing going on there, Georgie but thank you for your kind words." I snort out a laugh but it doesn't hold any humour. "Believe me, whatever there was, is over." I pat her hand that's resting on my arm and drop my hand back to the table top.

"I wouldn't be so sure about that." She winks and smiles at me, nodding her head towards the kitchen, before walking away. I watch her for a few seconds before looking up at where she was looking.

Sara's face is looking back at me through a small round window. It's not that easy to make out her features but I can tell it's her. I'd know her anywhere. I smile and salute her to let her know I know she's watching me and she disappears from the window. I can't help laughing, knowing that without a doubt she's more mad at me now than she was this morning when I left her.

My phone chimes with a message and take it out of my pocket to read it.

Leila: *umm I'll call you later*

Me: *everything ok?*

Leila: *yeah. Need to talk to Caleb*

Me: *are you safe?*

Leila: *I promise. I'll make it up to you*

Me: *cinnamon scrolls Leila.*

I wait a few minutes for her reply and when one doesn't come I send another one to her.

Me: *CINNAMON SCROLLS!!*

Leila: *yup*

I chuckle as I place my phone down on the table. I know Leila and I know I taught her how to fight, she may not have realised that's what I was doing at the time but it's the truth. Wrestling with me taught her how to get the upper hand with any guy bigger and stronger than her.

I'm brought out of my memories of our childhood when a plate clatters onto the table and someone takes the seat across from me. Perhaps I should be wary or surprised but I'm not. I had a feeling she wouldn't be able to resist for much longer, it's why I decided to wait her out.

"Why don't you take a seat, Sara?" Sarcasm dripping from every word. "Can I help you with something?"

Chapter Eleven
SARA

"Can you help me with something?" I splutter out. The nerve of this guy! We're both aware that he didn't stay here hoping to talk to his sister, not after we all saw them leave together and head to Caleb's place. You don't need to be a genius to work out what they're doing!

Even Betty and her friends knew better than to comment on that one. Out loud anyway!

"Yes. Is there something I can help you with, Miss Bankes?"

"Miss Bankes!" I'm sputtering again. I'm not this person, I never have been, not until Matthew fucking Phillips anyway. "I'm *Miss Bankes* now am I? That's fine, *Mister Phillips,* why don't you finish your food and get the hell out of my bistro?" I get to my feet, ready to walk away.

"Sit your gorgeous arse down." He commands quietly so that no-one else but the two of us can hear him, as he nods towards the chair opposite him. Sit down! Who the fuck does he think he is? He can't make me do anything! We're not together anymore, he walked out on me, not the other way around. My ridiculous body moves without my permission and starts to actually sit in the chair, before I realise its betrayal! When I *do* realise, I stand up quickly and cross my arms over my chest.

"No, I have work to do. Especially now that your sister has done a runner with her new man." I point my chin in the general direction of Caleb's house. "I guess screwing the boss has it bonus', it's just a shame that there aren't any single Drake siblings now." I know I'm pushing his buttons and when I see the muscles in his jaw clench, I start to wonder if I've pushed too hard but he started it.

And now I sound like the child I keep accusing *him* of being!

"If that's what you want, you're free to go for it." He says through gritted teeth.

"I don't need your permission to do *anything, Matthew.*" I make sure I emphasise the last two words and knowing what me calling him by his full name does to him, I smirk a little as his eyes narrow. "If you clench that jaw of yours much tighter, Matthew, you're going shatter your teeth."

"You know what, Sara? You're right, I just might and I know you said it to get a reaction out of me, still I let myself react." He places his hands on the table and then pushes back on it, slowly getting to his feet. "But you're right about one thing, *Ms Bankes*, you certainly don't need my permission to do anything. You can date or sleep with whoever you like and I know now, with great certainty that man isn't me. I'm done."

"Wait!" My voice is louder than I expect it to be. "Matt, please, don't go."

"Why should I stay, Sara? Give me one good reason why I should stay?"

"I -." I close my eyes and take a deep breath. I don't want him to leave, not like this but I can't tell him what he wants to hear either.

"That's exactly what I thought, Sara." Sighing, he stops beside me and rests a hand on my shoulder. "I just can't do this anymore. I want to be with you, Sara, I told you how I feel about you this morning and you said I was too young. Maybe we should take the chance to make a clear break and move on."

"But I -." I stammer out but I still can't finish my thought.

"I know, Sara, truly I do." He squeezes my shoulder gently and then drops his hand to his side. "You're not ready and not just for me but for anyone. It's not that I'm too young or Leila's brother, they're all excuses, I understand that now but I can't be your 'fun time guy' or your mistake any more. It hurts too much, Sara."

"That's not what or who you are, Matt, I swear." Panic rises from the pit of my stomach, into my chest.

"Right now, I am Sara and I love you too much to stay. I love *me* too much to stay, Sara. I won't be anyone's back up plan or secret fling. You use Leila as a shield and I'm done with it. I know I said that this morning before I left you to come here but after everything that happened here today and the way you stood so close to *me* in the tasting room when Leila and Caleb were answering questions. Well, I thought that you needed me but you don't, do you? You call me young and immature, Sara but in reality, you're the one who isn't very mature. You've pushed away guys forever, me included because you think that's safer. That'll be easier on your heart but you're breaking mine. I respect myself more than that and that's why I need to leave. I love you Sara, I probably always will but we're over."

I don't know what to say, so I say nothing and that seems to confirm everything he needs it to. I don't watch as he leaves Vines and myself behind. I don't get up from the table either. I watch him walk to his car, get in and drive away.

For the second time today, I've watched the man that I love drive away from me and I realise that I haven't just broken his heart, I've broken mine as well.

The coffee that I set down on the table for him goes cold and the muffin just sits there, mocking me.

"Hey, Sara." Georgie's soft voice beside me makes me jump. "Sorry, didn't mean to scare you but we're starting to clean things up. Did you want us to do anything specific?"

"No. Just close up and leave, Georgie. I'll clean everything up and then get a start on the things for the morning."

"Are you sure?"

"Absolutely." I smile up at her, knowing that my eyes are shining with tears, not happiness. "Get out of here and enjoy your weekend, what's left of it anyway."

"I can send everyone else home and stay to help you out."

"No, I can do it myself." I can see she wants to say more but I cut her off because I need this time alone. The kitchen will be cleaner than it's ever been and the dough will be kneaded within an inch of it being unusable but I need this. "Honestly, I want to do it and well, Leila isn't coming back. I wouldn't ask to her to even if I needed her to."

"She'd understand."

"I know but I want her to enjoy being with Caleb. She's loved him from the first day they met, even if she didn't let herself in on the secret, I knew. I've always known, so I'm happy for her, for both of them."

"That's not what I meant." Georgie raises an eyebrow at me. "I meant that she would understand about Matt."

"I have no idea what you're talking about, Georgie but Matthew Phillips is a free agent, he can do whatever he pleases."

"I don't think he wants to, Sara. He looked pretty upset when he left here earlier and I think he's pretty happy for his sister as well, after he got over the initial shock, anyway."

"He was just upset that he couldn't stay to eat his muffin and finish one of the best coffees in town." I smile again and push myself up from the table. I start to clean up the dishes left behind when Matt walked out but Georgie stops me.

"I've got these, why don't you head back to the kitchen and get started?" I nod my head, not in the mood for an argument. I've had more than enough of those for one day!

When I turn around I realise that Georgie and I are the only ones left in the place.

"Everyone left?" I ask, already knowing the answer. The place is empty. It's also clean.

"Yeah, a while ago." She lifts the dishes up and nods her head towards her sink near the coffee machine, before leaving me to go do her thing.

I make my way to the kitchen and start working. I mix and knead all kinds of dough. I prepare mixers so that we can come in, in the morning and just add wet ingredients. A couple of hours later, I almost have a heart attack when Georgie comes into the kitchen.

"Sorry." She laughs as I hold a dough crusted hand over my heart!

"No, I'm sorry. I was in another world, just getting the job done and I admit, I forgot you were even here. I'm used to either doing this alone or working silently beside Leila to get it all done."

"I could tell and I'm sorry, I didn't meant to scare you but I couldn't think of an easy way to let you know I was still here."

"Yeah, there wasn't an easy way, whatever you'd chosen to do, it would have made me jumped." I laugh because it's true, once I'm in the zone, not much can get through to me. "Kneading and mixing is very soothing and meditative for me. I relax and just let things happen."

"I've noticed that both you and Leila are like that." Georgie smiles kindly at me and I remember that she saw what happened today and my own smile fades. "Come on, if you're done we can walk out together."

I look around and decide that she's right. It's time to get out of here, even though I don't feel like going home and sleeping in the bed that Matt left me in this morning. I have to do it eventually and now that I've stopped moving, I'm feeling exhausted.

"Let's get out of here. Just let me wash up a little."

I go into the changeroom and clean up a little. When I come back out with my handbag and keys, Georgie has turned off the main lights and the security lights give the bistro a weird glow.

We head out the door and lock up behind us, neither of us saying a word as we walk to our cars that happily appear to be parked close together. I'm surprised when she pulls me into a hug.

"It will all work out, Sara."

"I'm sure Leila and Caleb will work out."

"They're not who I was talking about and you know it." She turns to walk to her car but as I open the driver's side door she stops and turns back to me. "He loves you, Sara, I want you to think about that. He's a good guy. A really decent man and he *loves you.*"

"That didn't seem to stop him from flirting with you." I say with a snort and then cover my mouth, horrified and wishing I could shove the words back into my mouth. Georgie doesn't seem to be offended though because she laughs loudly.

"He wasn't flirting with me, Sara. Well, OK, he *was* and I might have been flirting back a little but both of us were doing it for the same reason."

"And what was that?" I'm curious to hear her answer.

"To make you see what you're walking away from. I know it's not easy to walk away from him, Sara. I can see it on your face and in your eyes. Don't you think you deserve to be happy? That *he* deserves to be happy?"

"I do, that's why I'm walking away."

"Why? Because you assume that Leila won't approve? Or because you think the world won't approve? How about how you *feel*? Or how Matthew feels? Doesn't that count more than anything else?"

"Maybe."

"You're using Leila and the age difference as an excuse because you're afraid of being hurt, so you hurt others before they can hurt you. Have you ever thought that you're hurting yourself just as much it not more, than you're hurting him? You could be happy, Sara. You could fight to be happy. No-one is going to give a shit about the age difference if you don't. In fact, other people won't even notice if you don't announce it."

"Maybe."

"Just think about it, Sara, please?"

I snort out a small laugh. "When did you become a therapist?"

"Since I care about my friends and their happiness." A small, almost sad smile on her lips. "Just promise me that you'll think about what I said. He's a great man, Sara and he loves you but he won't wait around forever. You're going to have to fight for him."

I promise Georgie that I'll think about what she's said just to get away from the lecture.

I *know* Matt's a good guy, a great catch. I just don't know if I'm the best woman for *him* and by pushing him away, I'm trying to save both of us heart ache later.

The only problem is, my heart is breaking *now* and it really fucking hurts.

Chapter Twelve
MATT

Over the following days and weeks I avoid Vines and only visiting my sister there when I know for certain that Sara won't be there. I know that Leila has picked up on it and I know she wants to ask but she hasn't and I'm grateful. Instead, I join her at Caleb's house for dinner once a week to catch up. Every time I go there, there are more touches of my sister in Caleb's house and I can tell she hasn't realised that she's slowly moving in with him.

I catch Caleb's eye one night after a few weeks and the smile he gives me tells me everything I need to know. The bastard knows what's happening and he is loving it.

"So, when are you going to tell her?" I ask him as we stand out on their back deck, drinking a beer.

"Tell who what?" He thinks he hides his smirk as he takes a swig from his beer but I catch it.

"My sister. When are you going to tell her that you've been slowly moving her into your house?"

"I wouldn't do that!"

"Yeah sure you're not. I've seen the changes around here in the last few weeks. My sisters touch is in every room now and I've noticed that she's spending more and more time here and less time at her place."

"She does spend a bit of time here." He agrees with a slight nod. "It's just easier, what with Vines two minutes away."

"So, you're making my sister work more because staying here makes that easier?" I goad him.

"No. In fact, she's worked a lot less lately, any guesses as to why, Matthew?"

"No clue, Caleb." I'm sure I can take an educated guess but I don't want to think about her.

"Oh, I'm sure you can guess." He trains his gaze on mine but I continue looking out to the vineyard behind his property.

"This is truly a gorgeous view." We both know I'm trying to avoid what he's going to say next.

"It is but that's not what we're discussing."

"We're not?"

"No. We both know a certain assistant manager of Vines that is working too hard because she's nursing a broken heart."

"That's not my fault."

"I never said it was but you sure can fix it." He lowers his voice before continuing. "She's working herself to exhaustion, Matt. She's here before Leila can even get over there and she's pushing your sister out of the door in the early afternoons. She working until she's ready to fall asleep on her feet, just so that she doesn't think about *you*."

"I'm sorry she's working too hard, Caleb but you're her boss, as is Leila, you both have more power over what hours she works than I do." My voice is quiet as well. "She made her decision very clear."

"I get that it might have sounded like she'd made a choice and felt it was the right one at the time but she's damn miserable, Matt and so are you. Why can't you both see that?"

"Maybe because we haven't seen each other since the day your relationship with my sister came to light. I'm not happy about her choice but it is exactly that, *her choice*. I'm not going to force someone to be with me when they don't want to be. I'm not that guy and I never will be."

"Fair enough." Caleb nods and then the two of us stand there in silence and finish our beers, staring out at the vineyard. "You want another one?" He asks, lifting his empty bottle of beer, as if I was unsure of what he meant.

"Sure." We both turn and walk back into the house, neither of us talking. As Caleb enters the kitchen ahead of me we can hear heated whispers and he stops in his tracks, causing me to crash into his back. "What the fuck dude?"

"Sorry. I think we should head back outside." He says, trying to turn back around, while trying, without any luck, to turn me back around as well.

"Thought you wanted another beer?" I have no idea what changed his mind and I'm confused, until I hear her voice.

"It's because I'm here."

"Oh." I don't know what else to say but I stop fighting Caleb and we both stumble backwards and almost land on the floor.

"Caleb!" Leila cries out.

"Matt!" Sara cries out.

"We're fine!" Caleb says as we both steady ourselves and he looks at me. "Sorry dude."

"That's OK, no harm done." What else am I going to say to him? "You don't have to keep us apart, Leila, we're adults, I'm sure we can behave like it." I tell my sister without looking at her best friend.

"I know but I didn't want to put either of you in a position where you had to behave like adults about your break up just yet." Leila's so apologetic and I know it's for my benefit because she knew without ever asking, that I was avoiding Vines like it had the plague.

"Well, there was no break up, Lei, 'cause there was no relationship, as you put it, so it's fine." I explain, still not bringing myself to look at Sara but I hear her gasp at my words and I can't help feeling like a prick for saying them. "What? It's true, Sara, you made that abundantly clear." I say, when I finally look her way. When our eyes connect, I see the sadness that Caleb told me about but I steel my own heart against them. She did this, not me.

"I'm sorry, Matt." Leila says quietly.

"You're allowed to have your friend over to your house." I tell her, as I roll my eyes at her.

"No, I mean I'm sorry because I invited you both over for dinner on purpose."

"Leila." Caleb says my sister's name so quietly but he steps over to stand beside her, as if he has to protect her from *me*. I think he might need to protect her from Sara, not me.

"That's what we were arguing about when you guys walked in. She didn't know you'd be here either and I was trying to *explain* to her that *you* didn't know she was coming either."

"You weren't arguing, Darlin', you were whispering." Caleb chuckles.

"Not all arguing is in loud voices you know, Caleb!" Leila says to Caleb, then they argue good naturedly about what constitutes an argument and what doesn't, as Sara and I stand by quietly looking at each other.

Sara moves her head, gesturing towards the door leading back outside where Caleb and I just walked in from. "Want to talk?"

"Sure, lead the way." I wave my hand in front me and wait for her to do exactly that.

As I walk behind her to the deck that I just left, I can feel my body tense up and my mind goes into overdrive trying to work out what she wants to say. I thought we'd both said all that we wanted to weeks ago.

"Matt, I want to start off by apologising. I didn't know you'd be here and this wasn't planned at all. Not by me anyway."

I guess this conversation isn't going to go the way I'd hoped it might if she already apologising for something my sister did.

Chapter Thirteen
SARA

I'm surprised that Matt agreed to talk to me and followed me outside. So, when I turn around he's standing right behind me, I lose everything I had planned on saying. My mind goes blank and I just stare at him.

He's so fucking handsome, so sexy that I want to climb him and never put my feet back on the ground. I want to kick myself for pushing him away. I know why he walked away and I can't say I blame him but it still hurt like hell and I'm struggling with the why right now.

"Sara. Sara? Are you OK?" His voice brings me out of my daydream.

"Hmmm?" I can't find my words for some stupid reason.

"I asked if you were OK? You wanted to come out here and talk but you haven't said a word."

"Right. Of course!" I nod, like the idiot that I am and try to find the words I had ready in my head before I found myself face to face with the man that I now know, without a doubt, I'm in love with.

"Sara, if you've got nothing to say I'm going to head back inside to my sister and Caleb. It's a bit rude to be out here, at their home, when they've invited me, both of us, for dinner." When I don't respond right away, he turns to go back inside. Matt walking away from me once again spurs me into action and finally, I find my words.

"Matt, please, don't go." He stops mid-step but doesn't turn around to face me again. I take a deep breath to gather my thoughts and courage. I know, without reservation, that I won't get another chance to tell him how I feel. If I don't get it all out today, that's it. "Please, Matthew, stay and hear me out."

"Why? Give me one good reason *why* I should stay and hear you out, Sara. We've been here before and you couldn't give me what I wanted, what I need-ed and I think it might be for the best if that's how we leave it. Eventually, we might even be friends so that this isn't so tough on Leila." He lets out a huge sigh. "I guess I understand why she made that rule about me dating her co-workers. We proved her point for her, didn't we?" He takes another two steps towards the door and I need to stop him.

"I love you!" I say too loudly. I'm sure if Caleb and Leila actually *had* neighbours, they would have heard my declaration.

"What?" It's one word said so quietly I'm not one hundred percent sure he spoke but he *is* frozen in place. His hands gripped into tight fists at his side and his head hanging down, chin resting on his chest. He looks deflated and tense all at the same time.

"I love you, Matt." I repeat, this time my voice isn't as loud but it is more confident.

"Don't, Sara. Don't do this. Don't say it just because you think it's what I want to hear because honestly, I can't do this anymore. My heart hurt when I walked away from you, it's not even close to being repaired, so I know I can't survive this. If this is you telling me what you think I want to hear so that you get what *you* want, please just *don't*."

"Matthew, look at me, please? I don't want to talk to your back." For a little bit, I don't think he's going to do as I ask but slowly, ever so slowly, he turns around until he's facing me. When I finally get a good look at his face again, I wish that I hadn't asked him to turn around. All I see is pain, anguish and hurt. Knowing that I'm the one who put all of those feelings on his face hurts *me*.

"Are you happy now? Now that you can see the hurt that you've caused, the pain. Sara, please, let me go." I step forward and raise my hand to touch his face but he flinches back from my touch, so I drop my hand to my side. I take another step closer to him and he takes two back. "Stay where you are, please. Say what you have to say and then I'm going."

"I'm sorry Matt, I didn't think about how much I was hurting you."

"Yeah, well, now you know."

"I do but I hope that I can make it up to you. You know, over the next few decades. Together, if you'll have me." I smile at him but he's not looking at me, he's staring out at the vineyard beyond the back fence. "Matthew. Look at me, please. I know I hurt you but I need you to hear me and understand what I'm telling you."

"What is it, Sara? Spit it out so that I can leave." His head jerks up so that his gaze meets mine.

"I love you, Matthew. I'm *in* love with you and I want to be with you. Forever if you'll have me." I smile at him and rest my hand on his bicep. My smile broadens when he doesn't pull away from my touch. My happiness is short lived however and I can feel the tears well in my eyes.

"I won't. Have you that is." I can't help the gasp that escapes me. I can't believe that he is being this cruel.

"Matthew Patrick Phillips! I've never know you to be so cruel!" Leila says from somewhere behind her brother and I can only assume she was listening at the door. I hear heavy footsteps and then Matthew spins around, turning his back on me, I know Leila is standing there. "If Ma was here, she would be so disappointed in you right now."

"Well, she's not and you want to know something else? I don't care what you or Ma would say. I'm the one who put himself out there for this woman, your best friend. I'm the one who was willing to face *you* and tell you about *us*. And I was the one who told your best friend that I loved her and do you know what she said to me? Well, do you?" I've never heard Matt raise his voice but he's yelling right now and Caleb steps forward, ready to protect Leila from her angry brother. "Of course you don't because no-one's asked *me* about any of this. *My* feelings don't seem to matter. I'm not *enough* for her, Leila. I'm too young. I'm your *little* brother. I. Am. Not. Enough!" He's yelling now and all worked up. I can see how deeply he's breathing from here, by the rise and fall of his chest.

"You *are* enough, Matt. More than enough!" I yell back. "In fact, perhaps you're too much. Too fucking good for a girl like me. Who knows!" I can feel the tears sliding down my cheeks but I don't wipe them away. I want to feel them, I need to feel them.

"Sara Jayne Bankes, stop it! You're the best damn person I know and the best friend I've ever had and if this idiot brother of mine can't see the good in you, then he's the one with a problem, not you!"

"Leila, Darlin', calm down." Caleb pulls her into a gentle hug, her back to his front. "I think we need to go back inside and let these two sort this out. It's none of our business, Darlin'." He says it quietly in her ear but we can all still hear him. Leila sags against his chest and I know she's giving in to him and our situation.

"Fine. You two are idiots if you can't see how much you love each other and work this shit out." She says, looking between the two of us a few times. "But I'll love you both either way." Then she lets Caleb guide her back inside, closing the door behind them.

"Why? Why should I give you another chance to break my heart all over again, Sara?" He spins suddenly and catches my gaze in his, then takes two steps closer to me. It takes everything in me *not* to step back to get out of his way but I stand my ground. This is it, I know it is. This is my last and only chance to win him back. To have the love of my life back.

"Because I love you with everything in me and not being with you these past few weeks has almost killed me. I worked every waking hour just so that I had something other than missing you to think about. I needed to work myself to the point of exhaustion so that I could actually sleep at night. I stayed here more often than not, or in one of the cabins that Caleb has been doing up for visitors to stay in. Why? Because if I went home, I had to sleep on the couch and that fucker isn't very comfortable because if I slept in my bed all I could smell was you, us and it hurt. It physically hurt and then I couldn't sleep. All I could do was cry. I knew when you walked out the door that I was wrong. I've loved you for months, I just couldn't admit it. To myself and certainly not you. Why? Because the last time I let myself love anyone, it almost killed me, literally. He almost *killed me,* Matthew. And I know, logically, that you won't do that. That you would never intentionally hurt me, physically or emotionally but I had to get in first. I had to protect myself. I always protect myself from everyone, just ask Leila. I didn't even let *her* in for years either. I fought it, what was, is, between the two of us but I'm tired Matt. I'm tired of being alone, of being lonely. I'm tired of not having love because I'm scared. I'm so fucking scared, Matt." Tears are streaming down my face and I let them. I can't let anything hold me back anymore. "I'm scared that if I let you in, you'll hurt me more than he ever could have."

"I would never hurt you, Sara." Matt says as he gathers me in his arms.

"Can't you see, you already have? If you walk away now, you *will* hurt me but I will understand. I just, I need you to know that I love you. I've loved you almost from the first day we started seeing each other and it scared the hell out of me. No matter what happens between us today, I will always love you. Even if we both move on, there will be a corner of my heart always devoted to you and only you."

"You'll never have to find out what it's like to live without my love, Honey, I promise." His voice is quiet and I can feel it vibrate in his chest, against the side of my face.

"What?"

"Sara, I've loved you since the day we met. Not the first time we went out on a date or went back to your place or any of that stuff. I have loved you since the first day I walked into Vines and saw you there, with Leila, laughing at something. You were so full of life, that I couldn't look away. Why do you think Leila warned me off you? She saw it. She knew it then, just like she knew it now."

I pull back but don't step out of the circle of his arms. I just need to look in his eyes for a few minutes so that I can *see* that he means what he's saying.

"So, what does this mean? What does it mean for *us?*"

"It means that there's no more bullshit between us and we make this work. You're mine and I'm yours. Forever."

"Are you sure?"

"I've never been more sure of anything in my life." He kisses me, deeply and thoroughly. "I love you Sara Bankes."

"I love you, Matthew Phillips."

"Fuck me." I laugh because I know he means it, I know what it does to him when I call him Matthew.

"Definitely later." I promise. He opens his mouth to speak but groans in frustration when a cheer of happiness sounds behind him.

"See, Handsome, I knew they could get their shit together."

Epilogue
MATT

After Sara's almost public declaration of love, we moved pretty fast. Not as fast as Leila and Caleb once she realised she was basically living at his house but pretty damned fast. When Leila found out I knew that Caleb had been slowly moving her into the house, she was pissed at *me* but not *Caleb*! Apparently, it's my job as her brother to tell her these things. If I'd thought she didn't want it or that he was being malicious, then she would have known.

As for me, I discussed the moving in together thing *with* Sara because I'm a grown up and I wanted to prove to a certain someone that I wouldn't behave like an idiot like my likely soon to be brother in law.

The conversation went a little like this:

"So, Sara, what do you think about living with me?"

"I'm all for it."

"Really?"

"Absolutely."

"Would this happen sometime this century?" I'm joking as I ask her the question, although she does laugh at it.

"It could be arranged *much* sooner than that, Matthew." She tells me as she straddles my lap and taps her chin. "How about as soon as we find a house we both like?"

"Are you sure?" I stumble out.

"Absolutely. I wouldn't mind a house closer to work, so that I have less travel time. If that's OK with you?" I nod in agreement, as I try to wrap my head around not having to talk Sara into the idea of sharing a home with me. "Caleb offered us one of the cabins permanently at Drake Wines but I'd rather not live out on the 'compound'." Her laughter is light and bright.

"It's a bit like a compound, isn't it?" I ask completely distracted.

"Yeah. Oh, you didn't want to live there to be closer to Leila did you? Because we can discuss it, I don't want to take it out of contention if you'd rather live there. I just think there are too many people out there as it is and while I'd love to be closer to work, that seems a little too close. You know what I mean?"

"No, that's too close to Vines and Leila, honestly." I agree.

"I agree but I guess I should have asked you first. Sorry." She leans down and kisses me. It was supposed to be quick and light but once I get her lips on mine, I can't let her go that quickly. Instead, I deepen the kiss because I need it. I need the reassurance that she's real, that she's here and agreeing to live with me! "Whoa! That was something else cowboy." She says pulling back from my lips and breathing heavily.

"I love you Sara." My hands tighten on her hips to stop her from moving.

"I love you too, Matthew." I growl and in one swift movement, I stand up bringing her with me. She has a choice, she can either wrap her legs around my hips or she can drop her feet to the floor. Thankfully, she wraps her legs around me and her arms around my neck.

I carry her to the bedroom and throw her on the bed.

"You. Are. Mine." I tell her, as I strip my t-shirt up over my head.

"Yes. I. Am." She smiles and reaches up for me. "Now, come here and fuck me." I don't need to be told twice and I start to strip her out of her clothes.

"Hey guys! I hope you're decent?" Caleb's voice travels through the house, my sister's much quieter voice talking to him. I growl at his shit fucking timing but Sara laughs and smacks me on the chest.

"This right here? It's the only reason I need to *not* live out at Drake Wines." I grumble as I put my top back on. "Get yourself dressed and I'll go out there." I nod my head towards the *open* door of our bedroom.

"OK." She agrees through her laughter. It's not funny, I tell her as I adjusted my still hard dick in my jeans, which cracks her up more. I roll my eyes at her and walk out the living room.

"Can I help you with something or are you guys good with getting yourselves a drink and something to eat, as well as letting yourself into the house?"

"The door was unlocked." Caleb answers quickly with a smile wide enough to crack his face open. It wasn't unlocked and we all know it. "Did we interrupted something?" He drops his gaze to my crotch, making it obvious what he means.

"Enough, Caleb. I'm sorry, you wouldn't think he'd get this much joy out of this kind of thing anymore but he still does." She shrugs her shoulders in a, 'what can ya do', motion and I roll my eyes at her now. "There's no point asking for the key back either, he'll still get in."

"What can I do for you two?"

"We want to know if you guys want to join us for dinner." Caleb kind of asks.

"Why didn't you call first? I mean, it's not like we're close by. We could have been out."

"We can fix that if you move out to Drake Wines." Caleb informs me.

"We were just talking about that actually."

"You were?" Leila asks, shocked.

"We were and while we appreciate the offer, we're not living out on the compound, Caleb." Sara says as she enters the room and attaches herself to my side.

"It's not a compound Sara." I've never seen a grown man pout before but here we are!

"Of course not, Caleb." Sara says placatingly. "So, where are going for dinner?"

"You're not going to explain *why* you were talking about living together living out at Drake Wines?" Leila asks.

"Nope. So, dinner? Where are we going?" Sara smiles at my sister and Caleb. Leila's annoyed but she won't push for an answer from either of us, she's too worried about scaring Sara off and Sara works that to our advantage.

I love this woman more than I could ever explain to her!

SARA

Yes, we moved in together. No we didn't move out to Drake Wines but we're close enough that Leila and Caleb annoy us regularly! I mean that in the nicest possible way, obviously! Matt's sister is my best friend after all.

If someone had told me all those months ago when we started out as just fuck buddies that we'd be living together sooner rather than later, I would have made them go to a therapist. Yet here we are.

We've been in *our* house for almost a month and I thought that I'd start feeling a little claustrophobic sharing my space, not just with a 'someone else' but with my boyfriend but I'm not. I've been waiting for the feeling to hit and it hasn't. I feel like everyone else has been walking on eggshells waiting for me to implode as well but nope, I'm happy.

I love Matt so much and I'm fucking happy!

Am I waiting for the other shoe to drop and something to go wrong? Hell yes I am *but* I know that with Matt by my side, we can deal with whatever comes our way.

"No, Leila, we do *not* need you to come over." I hear Matt's voice as he walks back inside. "Leila, stop! We don't need your assistance, we are fine!" I can't help laughing at the exasperation in his voice.

"Everything OK?" I whisper, as he enters the room. He rolls his eyes in response but nods his head yes at the same time. "Leila, if you come over here any time before you're supposed to within the next week, I will physically remove you myself." I don't hear her response but I can imagine exactly what she said to her brother.

"This situation is one of the very valid reasons not to live out here. It's too close to work and Leila can't even manage to take a week off without wanting to come over here and check on things." I smile at him.

"She's worried we're having sex on all of her work surfaces." He smiles as he stalks towards me.

"Why on earth would she think that?" I ask as his arms wrap around my waist.

"I have no clue but we shouldn't let the opportunity slip by." I can feel his smirk, as his lips gently touch my neck.

"Georgie will be here any minute."

"I guess I better be quick then."

"Just what every woman wants to hear." I can't help laughing.

"So, it's true then?" Both of our heads snap up to find Georgie smirking at us.

"What's true?" I ask.

"Leila just called and asked me to clean down and disinfect every surface in the kitchen because, and I quote, 'I just know those two are having sex all over the place in there.' I tried to tell her you're not but then I walk in here and find you two like this."

"We're not and we haven't had sex in the kitchen." I reassure her.

"That's very specific and now I feel the need to clean every other surface in Vines!"

"That might be a wise idea." Matt says, seriously and I want to be mad at him but I can't. "I can help you with that."

The two of them head out of the kitchen, I listen to their bantering until it fades away to barely a murmur and laugh.

I love my life. I never thought I could be happy like this. I never thought I could find friends and make them my family but I have.

Oh and I love Matthew Patrick Phillip's with everything I have.

The End!

A BONUS
Drake Wines Happily Ever Afters
JULES

I've been around the Drake siblings since well before their parents died in a terrible car accident and I have to tell you, I have enjoyed watching them all get their happily ever after's. No more so than Logan Bishop-Drake, obviously.

Sitting here on the back deck of the main house on Drake Wines that Makenna and Brady live in now, I take my time to look at each and every family member, new and old, here.

Makenna and Brady are here, obviously, with the twins and their youngest daughter. After everything they went through to get pregnant, I am so happy for them! They decided when Gabby was born that their family was complete. Watching the kids grow up alongside each other is pure joy.

Savannah is the oldest and takes her role seriously. She's protective over all of the Drake cousins but none mean more to her than her little brother. We adopted Jax a couple of years after we got married and Savvy doesn't see him as anything except her brother.

I give thanks to Lori every day for this amazing, beautiful and kind hearted girl that she raised for the first few years of her life.

Leila and Caleb got married a few years ago and Makenna was worried that they were having the same issues that she'd had getting pregnant but in reality, they weren't trying. They wanted time to just be them, together and I respect them even more for it.

Caleb has spent a lot of time and effort, getting Drake Brewery up and running and it's doing brilliantly. Meanwhile, Leila has been working hard with Sara to get Vines right where they wanted it. The two of them bought the

Drakes out and joined together to make Vines their own, while also joining with Drake Wines and Drake Brewery perfectly.

Sara and Matt are still living together and enjoying life. Everyone, including Leila and Matt's mum, Kim have stopped asking them when they're getting married. They seem to be content just the way they are and won't be pressured into marriage or starting a family for that. They've got their own path and I'm the last one to tell anyone that they have to go the traditional path.

Me? Well, Logan and I are happily married. Caleb likes to remind us every chance that he can, that we're nauseatingly happy. After everything we've been through to get here, I don't care how sickly sweet we might appear to others. I know Caleb is only teasing us but it still tugs a little at my insecurities sometimes.

As for Logan, he's a little less grumpy and a *lot* happier. People didn't want to stop doing business with the Drake's when we got married or started a family, which is what he was afraid of. He's learned to relax a little bit, which makes us all happier. He's had no choice really, what with Jaspa the dog giving him unconditional love, the kids matching that and more and my unfaltering support and love.

While I sit here and watch them all interact, I can see it. The happiness is almost its own creature.

Logan is proud as punch of his younger brother and his success with the brewery. He's happy with his relationship with Leila even though he was nervous about it at first. He can see how happy they are.

I see him watching Makenna sometimes when he thinks no-one is watching and I see the emotion on his face. He's happy that she found Brady but he wishes he could have taken on some of their pain for them. He can't help it, he's a protector.

Then his face changes once again when he sees our kids and the love is obvious. I know he still sometimes worries that I think of Savvy as a burden. She came along so soon after we got married and was such a surprise for everyone but she's amazing. I've never not for one day wished she was anything but ours.

"Hey, Papa, are you OK?"

"Of course I am, Savvy. How could I not be? All of my favourite people are right here, laughing, playing and getting ready to sit down and share a meal. Life could not get any better than this."

Organised chaos breaks out, as Brady yells out that the food is ready.

As everyone descends on the table, jostling for the perfect seat, I smile because I know that Jack and Anna are looking down on their family and smiling. The big, loud and chaotic dinners are back in their house and they wouldn't have it any other way!

The End!

ALSO BY CHELLE PIMBLOTT:
BAREFOOT & DUMPED!

What would you do if your boyfriend dumped you at your parent's 30th wedding anniversary party?

LEXI

I know I should be more upset about my break up, but in reality there are only two reasons I'm annoyed. First and foremost, he did it before I could, and second, he did it at my freaking parent's party! Who does that? My ex douchebag that's who! Let's see how long I can drag out him picking up the tiny amount of crap he had at my place.

When my parent's insist that my sister and I leave their party to celebrate my break up, Lacey my best friend jumps on the chance and we're at our favourite bar drinking and dancing ourselves into oblivion, while sharing a table with a man that makes my skin sizzle. I have no time for someone new, even a one night stand, because I need to find me before I find another 'us'. I won't live to make someone else happy, or myself comfortable ever again.

GABE

Am I annoyed that Lexi hasn't called me yet? Yeah, I am, but I guess there could be a million reasons why she hasn't, and I'm just glad I was there to help her and her friends out. Happy to have made sure they were safe at the bar and then got home as well. I would hope someone would do it for my sister in similar circumstances.

When Lexi and I literally run into each other a week later, I can't believe my luck. It seems like the answer to all my prayers, until I realise she's freaked out because I know her name and she doesn't remember me, at all! As I watch her bolt, I know I have two choices, and I choose to walk away because I refuse to come across as any kind of creepy stalker. I've dealt with a crazy ex, and I won't do that to anyone. So, once again, I'm left without her number, and I decide to let it go. Let her go, but that's easier said than done.

When Lexi's ex plays a dangerous game, will Gabe be able to get to her in time to protect her?

AN EXCERPT from BAREFOOT & DUMPED!

Late in the week, I'm checking messages on my phone as I walk to get a coffee from my favourite café. I'm barely paying attention, but I have to pause at the door to let a lady leave so that I can enter. Only when I walk in what I think is an open doorway, I find a hard wall of muscle instead. The impact of our bodies knocks my phone out of my hand and with the quickest reflexes I've ever seen, an arm reaches out and catches it before it can hit the ground and smash into pieces.

"Oh my god! Thank you so much for catching my phone and I'm so sorry about walking into you. I should have been watching where I was going, but I had a one track mind heading into buy the best lemon slice in the world."

My hand is still resting on the solid wall of his chest and I feel the rumble of his laughter work its way through his body before it finally reaches his vocal chords. Then it's the most amazing sound I've ever heard. I can't hear the traffic or anything else. "No worries. Things happen, there was no harm done at all."

There's something familiar about him, his face is registering as someone I know, but I know without a doubt, if I knew him from anywhere I'd remember him.

"Thank you." I say, my voice barely a husky whisper.

"You're welcome Lexi." He says, handing me my phone.

"Excuse me, but can I get past please? I need to get to work." Asks the guy behind Mr Hazel eyes, who has been patiently waiting for us to move out of the way.

"Yes, of course," I say as we both move out of the doorway to let the guy through. That's when it registers that this guy knew my name.

"I was hoping we could exchange phone numbers this time ..." I don't let the guy finish. What the hell is he talking about and how does he know my name?

"This time? How do you know my name?" He opens his mouth to speak, but I hold up my hand to stop him. "No actually, please don't say another word. I'm going to walk away now and forget this ever happened and hopefully we can live the rest of our lives happily knowing that I didn't let the creepy guy kill me." I don't let him say anything, I just take off in the opposite direction to where I'm supposed to be heading. I didn't do it on purpose, I just wanted to get away from the guy I don't know, but who seems to know me. I mean he knew my name and asked for my number. Who the hell does that?

I hear him call my name from behind me, but I don't look back, he's freaking me the hell out and I pick up my pace. I'm not quite jogging, because well heels, but I am definitely power walking at this stage, until I find myself ducking very quickly into an arts supplies store. I make a quick circle of the shelves so that I don't look like a crazy person to the lady behind the counter and then smile at her on my way out.

"Did you need some help to find what you were looking for?" She asks as I reach for the door and I panic.

"No. Thank you, I'm fine." I reply quickly, knowing I look and sound as sketchy as hell. No pun intended. Without another thought I shoot out the door and look up and down the street to see if the guy has gone. When I can't see him anywhere I head back the way I came, but I don't go into the bakery like I had intended before I ran into 'the guy', instead I walk, at quite an impressive pace, to work. I can't wait to meet up with Lacey for lunch later and tell her about my stalker. She's going to want to call in ASIO or the FBI or the CIA. I can't think of any other acronyms for any more government organisations. I'm pretty sure the American agencies don't have any authority in Australia, but that won't stop Lacey from trying.

BUILT TO LAST: Book .1. Built for Love Series

Kami's spent the last few years getting her book shop up and running. When she needs some renovations done, she asks for recommendations, and the overwhelming response is, Harvey Carpentry. So, when she sees the truck with the Harvey logo, she takes the chance, and asks for a quote. The guy who turns around is James freaking Harvey, and he still takes my breath away, just like he did in high school. Kami should have connected the Harvey name to James, but it didn't even occur to her.

James is working hard to distance himself from his father's reputation, but it hasn't been easy. Even as men employ him to work in their homes, they warn him to keep his hands on the job and off their wives. Then Kami Parker walks up to his truck asking for a quote and James can't believe his luck. Now that they're adults maybe she can see that he's a guy worth spending time with. Maybe even a lifetime?

AN EXCERPT from BUILT TO LAST

I close my eyes because, after the tension and electricity that was just zapping around us not 5 minutes ago, everything I say seems to have a sexual undertone to it. I'm not even trying, for the first time in a long time, but it sure does seem to be coming out that way. I clear my throat and go to speak again but Kami beats me to it.

"Did you *make* an apple pie ... for me?" She asks. Here I was thinking that she'd gotten past my cooking skills, apparently not.

"Yes Kami, I made an apple pie, from scratch, for dessert. For you, well yeah cause you're here but I also felt like eating an apple pie, so I made one."

"From scratch?" I slowly nod my head in answer to her question because I can't be bothered voicing the same answer, again. "Wow! Umm yes, please, can I have some cream on top?"

I groan at the double meaning and dish us both up a slice of pie with cream on top. I can't even look at her, the thoughts that are rolling around my head, if I look at her I'm sure she'll be able to read my mind and go running out my door. Then I'll have lost the only chance I have with this beautiful woman. I've waited so long to have this chance, an opportunity to prove to her that I'm not as bad as everyone thinks, I can't get ahead of myself. It may have been a mistake to cook dinner for her and bring her out to my home, but even if it is, I wouldn't change it for anything. Well, except maybe an overnight stay with her, which included me getting to do all the things I want to with her.

Her groan snaps me out of my head and makes my cock instantly hard. When I look across the table at her, she's got her eyes closed, and she's licking her lips. My spoon is hovering somewhere between my bowl and my mouth, while I watch Kami take another mouthful of my apple pie to her mouth, open wide and moan again as she closes her mouth around the spoon. Fuck me, she's killing me, but what a way to die.

Her eyes open as she tells me, "Holy heck James, this is delicious. I swear it's the best thing I've had in my mouth in, forever." Then she realises what she's said as my jaw drops to the table and the cream starts to drip off my spoon. I should have changed out of my jeans, there isn't enough fucking room in them to eat dinner with this woman. "I, ummm, didn't mean that the way it came out. It's ... you're a really good cook James."

"Thank you Kami, coming from you, that means a lot." I say.

"Why? You don't even know if I can cook, I could be really bad for all you know, I mean I *do* go to the café every day for lunch." She laughs, and it's become my favourite sound in the last couple of days. "Maybe next time, you can come to my house and I'll cook for you?" Her whole body freezes as she realises what she's just said, and her spoon clangs back into her bowl.

"That's a deal Kami. Next time it's at your place and you're cooking for me." Without another word about it, I pick up my bowl and hers and take them to the sink. "Let's look at the plans I drew up for the renovations shall we?" It seems like it might be a safer subject right now and it should, with any luck, help my hard on become less hard!

BUILT FOR TROUBLE: Book .2. Built for Love Series

Can Katy forgive Joe's past behaviour to move towards a future together? Does love win over friendship?

Joe made Katy's best friend's life hell when they were at High School, but even then, there was still something that always drew her to him. When they start seeing each other at a local café where they both go for lunch, and share a table to, 'save space', they get to know each other as adults, and they like what they see.

When Joe asks Katy out for dinner, a date is set. One that neither of them ever saw coming. Especially given their past, but sometimes things happen for a reason. The draw to one another is electric and unrelenting .... unforgiving.

When Joe explains his reason for giving her best friend so much grief, something even more shocking is revealed in the process.

Can their relationships survive all the pain and grief that these revelations cause? Will love win in the end? The love between a man and a woman. The love between friends?

AN EXCERPT from BUILT FOR TROUBLE

"Does this dress of yours have a zip or buttons or can I just pull it off your body honey'?" I growl in her ear, as my hands wander all over her back trying to find how I can get her out of the damned thing.

"Mmmm." Is all I get out of her as she continues teasing my nipples and kissing along my jawline.

Kissing up her neck I ask in a husky whisper in her ear," Katy, tell me how to get this thing off or I'm just going to rip it off you."

"Mmmm," she moans again, then she seems to shake her head for a second and says, "Zip. At. The. Side." She hisses out between breaths and kisses.

I don't know who designed this damned thing, but it wasn't with an idea of getting anyone out of it in a fucking hurry that's for sure. My hands run up and down her sides, trying to find the zipper so that I can put my hands , my mouth and whatever else I can get on this woman. The dress needs to go, now.

"Katy," I groan against her neck, "Babe, I need to put you down for a second."

"Mmmm." Is her only response. She looks delectable, with her head leaning back against the door, making her neck stretch out and all I want to do is lick it and nibble on it.

Instead, I let her leg fall off my hip and place her foot on the floor, my hand gripping her hip. My other hand pulls down the zipper of her dress letting it fall to her waist. I let out what can only be described as an animalistic growl, a vocal declaration of the desire that's coursing through my body.

"Joe." Katy's voice is soft, husky and full of her own desire.

"Yes, Katy?" I reply. "What do you need babe?"

"You, I need you, Joe. God, I need you everywhere Joe."

"Everywhere? How do I get everywhere baby?"

"I don't know, I just know what I need." Her hands are running through my hair, over my shoulders, grasping my neck and running her nails up and down my back. It's like she can't get enough of me and I sure as fuck know I can't get enough of her.

"I know baby, I feel the same way. I'm trying to get us there but this dress.."

Don't miss out!

Visit the website below and you can sign up to receive emails whenever Chelle Pimblott publishes a new book. There's no charge and no obligation.

https://books2read.com/r/B-A-FGVL-JTUSB

BOOKS 2 READ

Connecting independent readers to independent writers.

Also by Chelle Pimblott

Built for Love
Built to Last
Built for Trouble

Drake Wines
Vineyard
Sandy Cove - A Drake Wines Novella
Winery
Lori's Memories - A Drake Wines Novella
Brewery
Sara's Forever

Standalone
Barefoot & Dumped!

www.ingramcontent.com/pod-product-compliance
Lightning Source LLC
Chambersburg PA
CBHW070638120726
47909CB00004B/1486